Killer CONnections

A Sadie Sabatini Mystery
Book 3

Nicole Leiren

ISBN: 978-1-963705-23-2

Published in the United States of America by Harbor Lane Books, LLC.

www.harborlanebooks.com

Chapter One

Texas summers were hot. This fun fact surprised no one. After growing up in North Dakota and then travelling around the United States after college to carry out my own personal version of the Robin Hood story, I'd started a new chapter of my life deep in the heart of Texas in the beautiful little town of Wilson. Situated on a peninsula that jutted into Lake Amore, my first full year here convinced me everything was bigger in Texas, including the temperature. This time around, summer had taken over most of spring, and with June nearing its end, the beautiful state had redefined my understanding of the word hot.

The intensity of the sun during the day was too much for my favorite outdoor activity, kayaking. This explained why, at nine-thirty in the evening, one could find me sweating buckets as I glided across the glassy water. I arrived at the small cove tucked away just on the other side of a large outcropping of trees. The Sam Houston Forest surrounded a good portion of the lake, which offered little hideaways and beautiful views. While I didn't understand how, I'd learned this spot often provided a gentle breeze even when the rest of the world remained still under a heavy blanket of heat. It also offered a stunning view of the moon reflecting off the lake.

I waited as the cloud cover moved, allowing the shy moon to see its reflection. Wiping the sweat from my brow, the breath entering and leaving my lungs slowed as calm entered my soul, removing the final vestiges of the craziness of the day. I'd looked forward to this moment for hours, that brief moment when all aspects of the world around me fell into the proper perspective.

The interlude was brief as the moon returned to its hiding place behind the darkening clouds. A small light under the surface of the water caught my attention. I blinked a few times to make sure my vision wasn't reproducing the moon effect, but quickly determined the reflection of light stemmed not from above, but below. What in the world could be causing a light from under the water? Maybe the heat was frying my brain more than I thought.

The sound of an outboard motor roaring nearby drew my attention and made me double check the lights installed on my kayak to ensure boaters would be aware of me at night. Once all safety measures were confirmed, I refocused on the area of the water where the light had pierced the murky depths. Darkness had returned. The trickle of sweat making its way down the nape of my neck transformed into a lazy river, prompting me to leave this mystery for another day. A cool shower and an evening chat with Jeremy, the handsome game warden who had captured my attention from the moment we'd met, would be the perfect way to end the night. Maybe if I asked nicely, he'd share where he was taking me for our first official date tomorrow evening.

I stroked the water steadily on my way home, now anxious for that cold shower. Mother Nature had apparently seen fit to not only turn up the furnace in our little part of the country, but she'd also sent the rain far away. While our neighbors to the north endured dangerous levels of water being dumped in their lakes and rivers, between our heat and drought, the only thing starting to rise in our little slice of paradise was people's tempers.

Tying the kayak to my dock, I entered my lakefront home and thanked the good Lord for the marvels of air conditioning. A quick check of my phone indicated I had a couple missed calls from EZ, but no messages, which I found odd. Whatever was so important would have to wait as my desire to shower outweighed my natural curiosity about the purpose of her calls.

I'd barely showered, dressed, and grabbed a snack when my front doorbell rang. The clock showed it was a little after ten. The front door camera feed revealed EZ had apparently grown tired of waiting for me to get back to her.

Opening the door, I smiled. "Well, it's none other than Estelle Zimmerman. To what do I owe the pleasure of such a late-night visit?"

"Ha, ha, very funny. Now, are you going to invite me in? It's hot as blazes out here and my pigtails are getting curlier by the minute in this heat."

"Of course, come on in. Can I get you something to drink?"

"Water."

As I retrieved a bottle from the fridge, I noticed her giving my place a onceover. "What do you think?"

She shrugged. "I think it's a lot to clean."

"You're not wrong," I laughed and gestured toward the sofa. Compared to EZ's residence, an RV tucked away on a little piece of paradise in unincorporated Wilson, I understood where she was coming from. "Please, have a seat. I'm sorry I haven't returned your calls yet. I was out kayaking and then was in desperate need of a shower."

"I figured you were just avoiding me once you realized I'd learned your dirty little secret."

The thundering in my chest resounded loudly in my brain. I had plenty of secrets, though I wouldn't categorize them as dirty, or little for that matter. My secrets all had to do with my past...something I'd been trying diligently to move forward from. "You're going to need to be more specific." There, that was generic enough to acknowledge her fishing expedition without baiting the hook. It would be a rookie mistake to inadvertently share information. Given my thirty years on this earth, I no longer qualified as new to the game of life.

"All right, if you wanna play it that way, I'm game." She took another drink of water. "I saw you earlier this evening."

My eyebrows knitted together in confusion. "Out on the lake? That's where I spent most of this lovely Friday once the sun started to go down."

"I can't believe you're going to make me say it out loud."

"Say what?"

"Look, I'm not judging, but hanging out in plain sight with a married man is a great way to destroy the reputation you've been trying to build."

My brain apparently wasn't the only one affected by this heat. "What on earth are you talking about? I barely encountered a man today. I was at the shop until closing time. After that, I made a quick trip to my storage unit to select pieces for the new line of jewelry I'm featuring tomorrow, picked up my dinner order from The Club, ate it, and then headed out on my kayak. Other than the server who delivered the food to my car, I've not been within six feet of the opposite sex today."

Her pigtails swished with the shaking of her head. "Look, I have to be at work in less than an hour, so I'll cut to the chase."

Finally!

"I saw you and JB at the Flying V campground late this afternoon."

A million questions started running through my head, but none of them made sense of the accusation EZ had just tossed my way. "Maybe you're suffering from heat stroke. I don't even know where that is, and I have no reason to be in public or private with JB Nester."

"Look, I don't care one way or the other. You do you. As your friend, I wanted to let you know someone, besides me, saw you."

"Why were you there? I thought your outdoorsy desires were limited to finding a nice view of nature while you smoked your cigarettes."

As if to prove my point about smoking, her laughter at my statement resembled the crunch of gravel being driven over by a big truck. It was followed by a small coughing episode. "Not that it's any of your dang business, but I was visiting with Robert."

Robert Birmingham was at the top of the elite ladder not only here in Wilson, but also the surrounding area. Wealth, power, and prestige were often associated with his name and family. He'd been married to his wife, Dora Lee, for decades. He also had one weakness in life that I'd been able to surmise: Estelle "EZ" Zimmerman, a local legend at The Foxy Lady just on the outskirts of town. "What of your reputation?"

She chuckled, "People expect that kind of thing from me, but I don't care what people think. They already assume I'm the one corrupting him."

"And what of Robert's reputation, then?" The true nature of their relationship was always churning the gossip mill, but rarely did anyone ever speak of it in public. "Wasn't he worried? Dora Lee might tolerate him visiting you at your place of employment, but out in public where anyone could see?"

"It was his idea. As a matter of fact, he was pretty insistent. I figure no one Robert or Dora Lee would be worried about would be caught dead at a campground. Besides, you and JB were the ones acting cozy. Robert was more focused on the two of you than me," she pouted.

"I..." the pronoun was spoken with much emphasis, "...wasn't with JB today. Not sure what I can do to prove that to you. And why would Robert be so interested in whoever was with JB?"

EZ stood. "Like I would know. Anyway, I don't care what you do or who you do it with. I'm not going to say anything, but I can't promise Robert won't use that knowledge against you, if needed, in the future."

Robert and I had found ourselves on opposite sides of an issue many times since my arrival in town. While we typically played nice in the sandbox in public, more than one heated debate had taken place in private. I decided to state my case one last time, though, thus far, it hadn't been received by my intended target. "It wasn't me."

"I gotta run. Don't say I didn't warn you."

"Don't work too hard."

She laughed. "Never. I make them do all the work!"

With that parting shot, she left. I locked the door behind her with a sigh. There was really only one explanation for me being sighted in public when I was nowhere around. Though, even that explanation didn't make any sense. I picked up the phone and dialed my sister's number. It went straight to voicemail. "Sydney, it's Sadie. We need to talk."

Chapter Two

When the alarm went off Saturday morning, I was certain I couldn't have slept more than a few hours. Robert and EZ weren't my main concern. EZ would respect my privacy, and Robert (and his wife, Dora Lee) would only use the information if it served them well in the future. One didn't get to the top of all the ladders–financial, social, and otherwise–by being impulsive and petty.

No, what had me lying awake at night was not hearing back from my sister. Was she in trouble? If it was her meeting with JB, why? And, most importantly, why hadn't she called to let me know she was in town? None of it made any sense. We weren't super close anymore, but we weren't estranged, either. Our busy lives kept us from spending much time together, but we loved each other. And, to the best of my knowledge, she wasn't angry at me for any reason. Which brought me back to my first concern, that she was in some kind of trouble. I'd been on this merry-go-round of reasoning all throughout the night.

Those thoughts would need to be dealt with later. Now, it was time to get ready for work. My outfit was chosen carefully. It needed to be cool, comfortable, and chic. I'd been advertising for a couple of weeks now about a new line of jewelry featuring aquamarine stones. The pieces were handcrafted from Italy and included accents to complement styles ranging from casual to evening attire. I chose white capris with a pleated halter top that matched the color of the jewels being promoted. Silver jewelry and white strappy sandals finished the ensemble.

I opened my boutique, Tesoro, promptly at nine o'clock, excited about the day. This shop was my new passion. Items here featured hand-blown Murano glass shaped into everything from dishes to centerpieces, and jewelry. It was a tribute to my heritage and my appreciation for the beauty in life.

My first customer in the door was my best friend here in Wilson. "Morning, Kelsey. So glad you could stop in today!"

"I certainly couldn't miss seeing this new line of jewelry. My anniversary is coming up and Pete will be asking for ideas. Figured something from the new collection would serve as a great starting point."

Her smile as she immediately moved to the lighted display case warmed my heart. "The aquamarine colors will certainly suit your coloring and complement your beautiful auburn hair."

"You don't have to butter me up. You know I love your selections."

"I'm not using flattery to make a sale," I laughed. "I'm simply reminding my friend how beautiful she is."

Her cheeks flushed to a lighter shade of her hair. She was a confident woman, but like most women, she tended to have a hard time accepting a compliment. "Well, thank you. I appreciate that."

After giving her a few minutes to look over the new pieces, I jumped back into conversation. "Anything new to hit the rumor mill in the last day or so?" If Robert had shared his alleged sighting of me with anyone in the community, as a hub in the town gossip wheel, Kelsey would be among the first to know. She didn't typically spread gossip–well, except to me–but people tended to share with her. Maybe it was because they knew she'd keep their secrets. That thought reminded me I'd yet to trust all my secrets with her. I'd shared more with her than anyone, but I hadn't been able to bring myself to tell her everything. Not yet, at least.

"Besides conversation about the increase of drugs in the area, everything else is more harmless gossip. Most of it over the last day or so has centered around Denise and Alan. They've been seen about town this past week looking rather cozy." Her eyebrows waggled a bit as she shared.

I hadn't heard anything official about the drugs, but Emerson, a local teen who befriended me right from the beginning, had shared he'd witnessed multiple drug deals happening in his school. We were both trying to figure out the best way for him to handle that and still stay safe. Keeping the topic light, I replied, "Well, good for her. She's had the hots for him since I've known her."

"They do seem very happy. Only time will tell if it lasts."

"True. Hopefully, now that the thrill of the chase is over, she won't grow bored. Though, when she was such a staunch supporter of him in the last election, I began to think maybe it was more than a fleeting crush."

"Or an obsession," Kelsey teased.

"True as well. Thankfully, he was flattered by her interest rather than seeking a restraining order from the police."

Kelsey returned her attention to the display case. I noticed her gaze being drawn to a particular necklace. I made a mental note to send a picture of it to Pete with a suggestion that it would be the perfect gift for their anniversary. "I'm a little worried about JB," she shared out of the blue.

"JB Nester?" Not that I knew any other JBs, but this was the south and there could be more men with those initials. "What about him?"

"I'm not sure. He just seems...off."

"When did you last see him?"

"At The Club last night. Instead of sitting with his usual group, he was at a corner table with Lester Price. They both appeared to have the weight of the world on their shoulders and Lester looked like he'd been roughed up. JB was pretty earnest, and Lester was more agitated than a long-tailed cat at a rocking chair convention."

I couldn't help but laugh. "Well, that's a new one for me. But Lester getting in a fight doesn't surprise me at all. His ability to get along with others leaves a lot to be desired." The timeline in my head made it reasonable to assume this was after EZ and Robert had seen JB at the campground. "Did you speak with either of them?"

She shook her head. "I'd started to make my way over to him when Lester bolted from his chair and stormed out. Figured I'd wait before engaging in conversation. JB left a few minutes later."

"How weird. I wonder what's going on?"

"No idea." She gave me a smile. "But I'll see what I can find out. Any particular reason you're interested?" She added, "I know you're not a Lester fan. Have you and JB become friends?"

"Still not a fan, and more curious than anything else. I'm always suspicious anytime Lester is lurking around. I don't think I've ever seen him at The Club before."

"It's rare, but it does happen from time to time. Speaking of The Club, is that where you and Jeremy are having dinner tonight?"

The grin on my face at the mention of his name couldn't be suppressed. "He hasn't confirmed, but I think it's possible. I may have hinted about my excitement that scallops were back on the menu."

Kelsey's smile matched mine. "I hope you two have a wonderful evening wherever you're dining. I'm so glad you've been able to progress to this point, even though it has taken you longer than the average teenager," she teased.

It was my turn to blush. "Well, we had a few more things to work out than the average teen, but we've definitely made progress. Only time will tell."

"You make a cute couple. Don't blow it!" Kelsey bumped her shoulder with mine to emphasize her warning.

The smile on her face was contagious. "I'll do my best."

"All right, I need to be on my way. Domestic duties await."

"Make Pete help you!"

She laughed. "I would but he's working today. The firm is gearing up for a big case. Before you ask, he hasn't provided any details, just that it's a major deal and all hands are on deck to help with research and prepare the necessary pleadings along with other legal jargon I don't even want to understand."

"Okay, but if you get any juicy details..."

"You'll be the first to know."

After she left, I took a picture of the necklace and sent it to Pete before I forgot. Hopefully, he didn't open the text in front of Kelsey or my attempt to help him win major brownie points would be for nothing.

I grabbed my laptop from the back room. Until more customers arrived, I wanted to do a little research on JB and the company he worked for. Maybe something was going on at work that had him so upset. All right, I confess, my curiosity resulted more from what connection he, his company, and my sister might have. Then again, maybe it wasn't my sister. It's possible there was another woman who looked like us. There were lots of doppelgangers in the world. Maybe Sydney and I had one who was in town for a few days. Highly unlikely, but possible, I supposed.

I typed CellCo in the search bar. Immediately, thousands of results were provided. The company had a hand in multiple areas, from providing equipment for cell towers, to fiber optics for a variety of uses in multiple industries, and their less talked about division responsible for alternate sources of power. It was the last line of business that had riled up the fine folks in our area of Texas many times. Most notably, during the last local election. JB's opponents had campaigned that he was part of a business threatening the oil and gas industry from which so many in this area derived their livelihood.

Scrolling down, I scanned for any recent articles about them in the news. A couple months ago, there was an article detailing their application for government grants to fund research into improved batteries for hybrid vehicles. I'd just clicked on the article to read more when the doorbell chimed. Closing the laptop, I looked up and smiled at my guests. "Denise and Alan, to what do I owe the pleasure?"

Alan slipped his arm around Denise's waist. "We heard there was a new collection being premiered today. So, we had to check it out."

I moved over to the display. "Right this way. I'm showcasing the beautiful marriage of aquamarine stones with Murano blown glass. The settings are either gold, silver, or platinum."

The blue in Denise's eyes sparkled as she took in the display. "They're beautiful," she offered in a reverent whisper.

Alan looked at Denise with the same awe she had exhibited for the jewelry. I had to hand it to her. She'd set her sights on attracting his attention, and by all accounts, she'd been very successful. With the amount of effort she'd given to her goal, it was either going to turn out like this or she would have been arrested for stalking. It could have gone either way, but I was glad it turned out positively. "I'll give you two a few minutes. Let me know if you have any questions."

I watched Denise survey each piece before returning multiple times to an earring and necklace set. There was some whispered conversation before Alan smiled and nodded. His attention turned to me. "We'd like a closer look at these, please."

Removing them from the case, I handed the earrings to Denise. She held them up to her ear. "They complement your eye color and skin tone very well."

"They sure do," she gushed. "I love them."

"We'll take the set." Alan beamed.

"Fantastic choice! Let me get this wrapped up for you." We moved the party over to the counter and I began to write up the ticket. I knew it was old fashioned, but I preferred creating a handwritten description in cursive and then signing it. This gave them something to use for their homeowner's insurance and filled me with pride each time I transferred something of such beauty. As I finished up the transaction, I couldn't help but ask, "I know you both keep an eye on CellCo. Did they get the grant for developing the batteries for use in electric and hybrid vehicles?"

"Oh my, where to start?" Denise grinned. She loved sticking it to JB's company, though I wasn't entirely sure why. I didn't believe it was merely because they were looking into fuel sources outside of oil and gas.

"Usually, I would say the beginning, but it's probably best to start with the most recent information this time."

"Well…" She propped her elbows on the counter and leaned in. "Not only did their grant not get approved, there's also been a lot of controversy over their research into solid-state batteries."

"What kind of controversy?"

"For starters," Alan chimed in, "there are rumors they stole designs and research from Future Energy Sources–or FES, as they liked to be called–in West Texas."

"Since oil and gas is big in West Texas as well, I can understand why they'd prefer initials," I teased.

"Exactly, though I think most Texans understand we need alternative fuel sources, they just don't want to broadcast it, and they certainly don't want their main industry threatened."

"Speak for yourself," Denise added. "My family has been in oil and gas since the beginning. If it was good enough for them, it's good enough for me."

"I hear you," I quickly added, but I didn't go so far as to agree. "Does FES have a legitimate claim?" Rumors were one thing, but facts that could be presented in court were another.

"For obvious reasons, they're keeping a tight lid on it. Given their application for a grant to fund their research was denied, I wouldn't be surprised if they turned to other less legitimate ways to keep them going," Alan shared as he slipped his arm around Denise.

"You really think they would steal the research if they weren't given the money? That feels like a pretty big leap."

He shrugged. "Their history is filled with sketchy deals, rumors of misconduct, and financial challenges. Desperate people do desperate things."

Before I could ask anything more, my phone buzzed with an incoming call. It was my sister. "Will you both excuse me for just a moment?"

"Sure, I want to look at the plates to match my goblets. You don't mind, do you, honey?"

"No. We're spending the day together. This morning is what you want and..."

Denise blushed. "Tonight is what you want."

At that moment, I was very happy I had a reason to step away. "I'll be right back."

Once in the office, I answered the call, "Hey, Sydney."

"Hey, sis. What's up?"

"Are you in town?"

"Why do you ask?"

I didn't really think that question needed an explanation, but I decided I would cut to the chase. "Primarily because *I* was sighted being all cozy with a married man yesterday evening at the Flying V Campground. And, in case you're wondering, I don't even know where that is!"

"Listen, I can't really talk about it right now. Work is breathing down my neck to fix a huge PR problem. I promise to come for a visit soon."

Sisters could be so very annoying. I felt like I'd been

repeating myself a lot over the past twelve hours or so. First with EZ, now with my sister. "Sydney, are you in town?"

"Love you, sis. Talk soon."

And with that, she was gone. My sister was one of the first subjects I'd studied to learn about human nature. I wanted to understand what made her tick, mostly so I could annoy her when we were kids. One didn't have to be an expert to know she was being evasive. Which told me, even if she didn't, that she was in town and she had been with JB last night. The question was...why?!

Knowing I'd have to ponder that later, I moved back into the main retail area.

"Everything okay?" Denise asked, the concern on her face evident.

I needed to get better at masking my feelings, especially where family was concerned. I waved my hand in dismissal. "All is well. Just some minor family issues."

"All right, I'll let it go for now as we have lunch plans, but let me know if you need to talk."

"Thanks, Denise. I appreciate you." I handed them the ticket and their package. "And your business," I added with a smile.

Alan took the package and handed it to Denise. "Happy anniversary, baby."

In response, she wrapped her arms around him and placed a romance book worthy lip lock on him. I averted my gaze and was thankful no one else had come into the stop to witness this. Though, I supposed it could be good for business. A glossy photo of these two with the caption: *Men, wanna make your lady this happy? Shop Tesoro!*

"See you later, Sadie."

"Later, Denise. Bye, Alan. And happy anniversary." Though, I had no idea what it was the anniversary of as they'd only been together a short time. But hey, business was business, right?

The rest of the afternoon passed by quickly with patrons, both new and old, visiting the shop. I confess, my heart swelled at how accepting the community had been of both me and the beautiful treasures from my father's homeland. It might have taken a little longer than I'd originally hoped, but anything worth having was worth working for. One of the many lessons my parents had instilled in me.

The air felt unusually heavy when I stepped outside in the early evening hours. There was a gray haze blanketing everything and a stillness that seemingly suppressed one's ability to breathe. I forced a deep breath and was rewarded with a coughing fit. What in the world was going on? I'd not been to Texas for very long, but this weather phenomenon felt strangely out of place.

A small part of me hoped the overcast nature of the sky meant the possibility of rain and a cooling off period, but I feared that was not the case. Not wanting to venture another deep breath, I closed my eyes and drew in air through my nose, focusing on the scent. My nonna on my mom's side grew up on a farm and always said if you really paid attention, you could smell the rain in the air.

The scent of the sky did not relay the promise of fresh, cool rain. Instead, it left an acrid taste in my mouth. The urge to cough again forced me to seek refuge in my truck. The air conditioning did its job and cooled my body and senses. I decided this puzzle could be further solved from inside my house.

The drive home was only a few short minutes away. The normal life signs on the streets were absent. Even the deer appeared to be hiding out. How very odd.

My neighbor was standing on his front porch, glass of wine in hand, when I pulled into the drive. After parking in the garage, I decided to brave the outdoors for another minute to say hello. Standing in my driveway, I waved, "Good evening, Mr. Crossman."

"You're making me feel old, stop it." His voice was gruff, but the slight upturn at the corners of his mouth indicated he was teasing a bit.

"All right, how about Mr. Jerome, then?"

"No one called me Jerome but my mother and my wife when she was mad at me."

This wasn't the first time we'd had this conversation, but I always found it enjoyable. "What shall I call you?"

He chuckled. "Anything but late for dinner."

I joined in the laughter. He tried to play the grumpy old man, but inside he was a softy with a great sense of humor. "Fair enough. How about we settle for Jerry then?"

"If that makes you happy."

"It does." I paused for a moment as we'd now ended our routine conversation. "Hey, Jerry, what's going on with the sky tonight?"

He took another sip of his wine. "Can't say for certain but thinking fire."

"Fire?"

"Well, you don't have to believe me, but after working in a fire department for a stint, I think I know what I'm talking about."

"Of course. I wasn't questioning you, more worried about the forest surrounding the lake if that's the case." Jerry had worked in any number of professions over the years. As a matter of fact, there hadn't been one conversation we'd had about anything that he didn't claim to have spent some time doing as a profession. Since I suspected he was at least in his early or mid-eighties, it was reasonable to believe he could have held any number of jobs during that time. I'd certainly pretended to be an expert in lots of professions over the years.

"You should get inside. This air's not good for your young lungs."

"I'm heading in. For the record, I'm pretty sure this air isn't good for more seasoned lungs, either." Better than saying he was old, right?

"Last time I checked, you weren't my mother. Now, get on inside."

Once again, he tried to sound grumpy, but I knew his heart was in the right place. I stood at attention and saluted, "Sir, yes sir!" After too much wine one evening, he'd shared that he'd served our country in Vietnam. He wouldn't give details, but his haunted expression had told me all I needed to know.

"Sassy, sassy Sadie." He grumbled, but I could see the smile around the rim of his glass as he took another sip.

"Be safe, Jerry."

"You too."

My phone started buzzing the moment I stepped into my kitchen. "Hi, Jeremy."

"Hey, Sadie. Look..."

The pause said the words he struggled to get out. "You're getting called in because of the fire, aren't you?"

"I'm sorry. I was really looking forward to tonight."

Me too. "It's all right. I understand. Any idea what happened?"

"Not sure. Fire broke out at the far end of the lake, by your favorite little cove. The fire department will know more once they get the blaze contained. Right now, that's priority one. I will work to divert boaters away from the area to ensure their safety and keep an eye on the potential impact to the lake."

"Sounds like a lot of responsibility, and more danger than I want to think about."

"I'll be fine. Besides, it's all part of the job."

Typically, his job didn't put him directly in harm's way. At least, not like this. "I understand. Just, please be safe."

"Always. And Sadie?"

"Yes?"

"I promise to make this up to you. I know how important tonight was going to be."

Hearing him say the words out loud meant so much. As Kelsey had so gleefully pointed out, our relationship had progressed at a snail's pace. We'd had dinner together several times, but it had been more of a shared meal between friends. The delay to a more serious relationship was my fault. I couldn't–or, more aptly, wouldn't–share about my past. He was a straightforward, what-you-see-is-what-you-get kind of guy, so, to him, secrets meant a lack of trust. Recent events prompted both of us to look harder and consider there might be some room to bend. Tonight was to be the first opportunity to explore where this new understanding might take us.

Oh well, there was always another day. Today, the safety of the lake, the forest, and all the residents surrounding it was imperative. "I know, but I'm sure we can find a way to make it up to each other. Call me when your shift is over so I know you're okay."

"I have no idea what time that will be."

"It doesn't matter. Sleep is highly overrated, anyway."

His chuckle brought a smile to my face. "Overrated, but important. But I'll call and leave a message in case you don't answer."

"Thanks, Jeremy."

"Have a nice evening, Sadie."

We disconnected the call. Thoughts of my sister and what she had gotten herself and possibly me into promised to deliver anything but a nice evening. However, since there was nothing I could do about that situation until she clued me in or showed her face, I'd focus on what was in front of me. Slipping a bandana around my nose and mouth, I stepped out onto the back deck. The gray of the sky was darkening to an ominous black. Breathing would become more difficult the longer the fire raged. From what I could see with limited vision, Jeremy's assessment of where the fire started matched where the blaze was still raging.

The same area I'd been watching the moon from just the night before.

I stepped back inside and picked up my phone to send quick texts to Kelsey and Emerson to make sure they were okay. I'd just hit send when my phone rang.

"Hello, Mamma, to what do I owe the unexpected call?" My parents and I were creatures of habit and fairly regimented in said habits. We had a video call every Sunday evening. I would sometimes text them, but my parents preferred voice or video calls over quick, short messages. They claimed it wasn't very personal, but I suspected technology might be more a factor than anything else.

"I'm worried about Sydney. Have you spoken to her?"

For my mother to call and voice concern, something more had to be going on than even I suspected. "I spoke to her briefly yesterday. She has a big work thing going on. Do you know who the client is?" I figured that might help me narrow down some possibilities.

"Some company called CellCo. I'm not sure what her specific assignment is, though. She's been very vague, which means..." She let the statement drift off as worry filled the space between us.

"I know a little about that company. Let me make some calls and see what I can find out."

"I would really appreciate it if you could, Sadie. It's unusual for her to not return my calls. I even texted, but nothing. Before you settled in Texas, I accepted such behavior from you, but I still always worried."

It was true. Out of the two of us, Sydney had always been the more *normal* one. For her to have gone radio silent on our mother, something was wrong. "Don't worry, Mamma, I'll find her and make sure all is well. Trust me."

"I do, Sadie. Thank you."

As soon as the call ended, I dialed my sister again. Straight to voicemail. Once I found her and made sure everything was okay, we were going to have a serious talk. I looked at the clock. A little after eight. I wanted to go out looking for her, but I had no idea where to start. A check out the window confirmed the sky continued to darken with the smoke from the fire. Without any idea where to begin, going out right now would be a fool's errand.

There was one thing to try, but I'd never given it much credence. I was a woman who dealt in reality, not superstition. But desperate times and all...

I sat cross-legged on the couch and took a few deep breaths, exhaling slowly. Clearing my mind of everything else, I thought only of my sister. I would learn how viable our "twin connection" truly was. Focusing on our times together, I remembered all the fun we had as kids, the trouble we caused as teenagers, and then the distance between us as adults. Our lives had taken two very separate paths. Perhaps, that's why the connection had been fuzzy over the past several years.

Sadness filled my memories. How had I let this go on so long? I'd been so focused on helping others, I now worried I couldn't help the one person who was more like me than anyone else on the face of the earth.

A knock jolted me from my spiraling. I opened the door to see none other than the person of my thoughts standing in front of me, looking worse for wear. Before I could say anything, my sister pulled me into a hug.

"Sadie, I need your help."

Chapter Three

After getting Sydney inside and providing her with a glass of water, I needed some answers. "I want to help, Syd, but I need to know what's going on."

"Everything is so messed up. I was only trying to do my job."

"Helping CellCo with its public image?"

"How did you know they were my client?" Sydney asked with a slight hint of accusation. "Meddling in other people's lives still? I thought you'd given that up."

Now was not the time to debate my life choices with my sister. She had no idea how I'd spent my time over the last decade, so her comment went back to our youth. I'd always been a champion for the underdog, which she interpreted as unnecessary interference. She, on the other hand, had led the charmed life of a popular girl and cheerleader throughout high school. My opinion was that she'd interfered with other people's lives, but not in a positive way. We'd often argued about that detail throughout our school years.

Now, only moments after asking for my help, she'd made the jump from needing my assistance to accusing me of meddling. Guess old habits were hard to break. "For your information, little sister, our mother called earlier this evening. She was worried sick about you. She told me your client was CellCo. And if you want my help, you need to tell me what the heck is going on."

At my words, Sydney stood, rage flaring in the black of her irises. "You are older than me by like five minutes, so why don't you just let it go? For thirty years, you've been holding that over my head."

"Thirty years and five minutes to be exact." I grinned. I couldn't help it. Sisters had a tendency to bring out the petty in each other.

"Arrgggh! Can you be serious for just one minute? I'm in major trouble here."

My demeanor sobered. "How does helping your client put you in trouble? What has your employer said about all of this?"

"Oh, Perfect Media Solutions has instructed me to do my job and handle the situation. The problem is they don't understand the full nature of the problem and, apparently, aren't all that interested in hearing about it, either."

I gave myself major brownie points for not mentioning at this moment in time that the acronym for my sister's employer was PMS. It was too good to not use in the future, but now was not the time. "I'm interested, though. I want to help, but I'll be better equipped if you bring me in the loop."

"It was a mistake to come here." With a shake of her head, Sydney grabbed her purse, the water bottle I'd given her, and headed for the exit.

As she flung open the door, Chief Parker stood there, with additional officers standing behind him. "Ms. Sabatini, going somewhere?"

Realizing the mistake he was making, I quickly moved into view. "Chief Parker, what brings you here this late at night? Did something happen to Jeremy?" Fear laced every word as I couldn't imagine any other reason he would be at my doorstep. Though, it seemed overkill to bring such a strong police presence. How did they think I would react, even if it was terrible news?

"What in tarnation? There's two of 'em?" Deputy Matthews, my least favorite law enforcement officer, made himself known from behind the looming presence of the chief.

Other than a quick flash of astonishment across his face, Chief Parker made no other response to seeing two of me before him. "Chief, this is my twin sister, Sydney."

"An identical twin sister. Well, that certainly complicates things."

"Complicates what? How?"

"Well, I came here to arrest you. Well, one of you." He looked more confused than I'd ever seen him. "At least, I think that's what needs to happen here. Maybe I should take both of you in until we get this straightened out."

A cough from a couple of officers in the back of the group prompted me into action. "Please, let's step inside and get you out of the smoke." *And reduce the amount of gossip material for my neighbors.* I could only imagine what Jerry was going to say about all of this.

The Chief nodded, and all four representatives of law enforcement stepped inside. "Thank you, Ms. Sabatini."

"Of course. Now, back to this arrest business…"

Before I could say anything further, Sydney moved in front of me. "No need to take both of us in, sir. It's me you want."

"Sydney!" I shot her an annoyed look. She asked for my help and now she was just giving herself up. I really needed to understand what was going on here. "Want? For what?" I also wished we'd made better use of our time, not that it had been much. Having more information before the cops showed up was always beneficial, even if it was merely to get our stories straight.

Hearing Sydney's confession, Chief Parker moved forward with his cuffs in hand. "Arresting her for the murder of J.B. Nester."

J.B, murdered? That couldn't be possible! "Hold on a second, Chief. What do you mean? When? How?"

Before he could respond, Deputy Jake swaggered up to stand beside him. "Ain't too hard to understand. She killed him. We're taking her in."

There were teeth marks in my tongue to bite back the not so choice words I had for him in that moment. I chose only one, but I leveled him with my best glare. "Allegedly."

"I'm in no mood to listen to you two squabble. I'm here to conduct the necessary business and then we'll be on our way."

My mind was reeling trying to process everything. J.B. was dead and they thought Sydney killed him. They didn't know her like I did. She would never harm an animal, much less a human.

Without any resistance, Sydney turned around, put her hands behind her back, and waited for the cuffs to click into place. I couldn't stand by and let it happen. "Hold on a minute! Let me see the arrest warrant."

Chief Parker handed me the piece of paper. I scanned it and handed it back to him. "The arrest warrant is for me, not my sister." It was a technicality, but an important one.

To his credit, the chief only looked mildly flustered by this. "We didn't know she existed. Besides, she just clarified and surrendered."

My brain was whirling, trying to think of a way to slow this process down. My sister volunteering as tribute wasn't helping. She'd never been a hero, so why she felt the need to start now was anyone's guess. "Perhaps, but you have to admit this would provide a defense attorney a great amount of reasonable doubt to serve up to a jury. You've shown up to arrest me, but take someone who looks just like me…" I let the words hang in the air to see how he would respond.

"Let's take 'em both, Chief. That way we can be sure." Deputy Jake, the president of the Sadie Sabatini Hater's Club, piped up. I really wished I understood why he had such an aversion to me. It had been that way since the beginning. I also now regretted letting him inside my house.

After some tense moments, Chief Parker took the cuffs off my sister. "Your sister makes a valid point. We'd like you to come down to the station for questioning, Ms. Sabatini. If that's your last name, that is."

The relief crossing my sister's face eased my mind the tiniest of bits. "It is," she shared. "I'm happy to cooperate with your investigation, Chief."

He certainly wasn't used to that from me. "As soon as her attorney can be present," I added.

Annoyance flitted across his face, but he kept himself in check. "Then, she will have to be my guest until Monday morning. We might not be able to arrest her, but she's now wanted for questioning in a murder case. Given she doesn't live here, she presents a significant flight risk."

The man had a point. I didn't like it, but I also knew he had up to forty-eight hours to hold her without levying official charges. "Do you have accommodations to hold overnight guests?" I'd been in the local station a couple of times. They barely had what could be considered an interrogation room.

"I'll make sure she's comfortable. You have my word."

As much as I didn't want to believe him, I did. At his core, he was a good man who followed the rules–every single one of them to the letter, which often put us at odds–but he'd also gained my respect. "All right. Let me grab her a few things. I can come by to visit tomorrow?"

He nodded. "Of course."

I took my sister's now uncuffed hand. "Hang on, I've got some toiletries, pajamas, and a change of clothes for you."

I gathered everything quickly and put it in an overnight bag. I handed it to Chief Parker before taking Sydney's hands in mine again. "We're going to get through this. I have a great attorney on retainer."

"Yeah, 'cause she needs one," Deputy Jake scoffed from the back of the crowd where he'd retreated, earning him a glare from the chief.

I added my glare and an evil eye for good measure, but quickly refocused on my sister. "We'll figure this out." I squeezed her hands tighter. "Together."

She nodded. "Don't mention this to Mamma and Papà. You know how they worry."

"I'll do my best." I wouldn't lie to them, but I wouldn't volunteer the information without prompting.

This seemed to appease her. "Okay, Chief, let's go. I'll see you tomorrow, Sadie."

"You will," I promised.

I watched them lead Sydney to the Chief's truck. He opened the door, like a gentleman, and helped her in. The overnight bag was placed in the back. I was certain he would look through it before allowing her to take possession, but he wouldn't find I'd slipped anything in there except the items I'd indicated along with a picture of the two of us from when we were younger. Something to remind her of happier times.

Once inside, I fired up my laptop and sent an email to my attorney, Joseph T. Thomas III. He might see it before Monday morning, but if not, he would read it first thing that morning. And just in case he had court, I'd also call to make sure he could be present when my sister was officially questioned. In the meantime, I'd visit her tomorrow and learn whatever details I could to try and help her.

The wheels of justice didn't typically move very fast around here, a detail I'd been very appreciative of in the past. It wasn't that they didn't want justice, more that as a small town, they didn't always get priority for DNA results and other necessary requirements before one was arrested, especially for murder.

Since my sister had been seen on Friday evening with JB and this was only Saturday evening, the wheels of justice were breaking every known speed law in order for them to obtain an arrest warrant in such short order.

I grabbed a glass of wine and started pacing, trying to think through scenarios that would result in a potential arrest in around twenty-four hours. My first inclination was to call Jeremy and get his thoughts. Because we approached problems in two distinctly different ways (him typically following all the rules, and me taking a more liberal approach), we made a great problem-solving team. But that wasn't an option tonight. He needed to focus on his job and didn't need any distractions. His safety, as well as the safety of those on the lake and in the area affected by the fire, was more of a priority right now. I'd been solving problems long before he came into my life. I could manage a solo run at this.

One would normally assume there was a murder weapon which would serve as the incriminating evidence. However, my experience here had taught me that running the forensics on a potential item didn't happen overnight. Even given JB's status within the community, the murder would've had to take place late Friday night, and this was barely twenty-four hours later. The wheels of justice might turn that fast if the mayor or governor were killed, but a local businessman and former politician? Not likely.

My phone buzzed with an incoming call. A quick look at the clock showed it to be around ten. No one called me this late at night, which sent my worry alarm spiking. I found the phone on the counter in the kitchen. It was Kelsey. "Is everything all right?" I immediately asked her.

"Oh, thank God, you're okay."

Kelsey had obviously been worried about me, though I wasn't sure why. "I'm fine. Why wouldn't I be?"

There was a reasonable pause, longer than one would expect in this situation. "The rumor mill said you'd been taken away in Chief Parker's truck."

Talk about speedy. The rumor mill was moving at the pace of lightning and working overtime tonight. "That wasn't me, it was my twin sister."

Another long pause. Guess our friendly discussions hadn't delved into the inner workings of family situations yet. My fierce guarding of the private side of my life had been ingrained in me for over a decade. It was to protect those I loved. "Oh, I didn't know you had a twin sister."

"Surprise," I offered weakly. "I'm sorry, force of habit."

She sighed. "Is your sister going to be all right? What happened?"

Her tone possessed just a hint of annoyance. I didn't blame her. She'd been my best friend here in Wilson since I'd first moved here. She deserved better. I would work on being better. "She's been taken in for questioning in the murder of JB Nester."

"Oh my."

"Yes. Not good, I'm afraid." I paused. "Before you ask, the answer is no. I don't think she did it. I think she was working with JB, something to do with him and his job. She works in public relations. It's my understanding CellCo was her client." Hopefully, the sharing of all this additional information would soothe things over a bit.

"Oh, I imagine their public image would need a little help."

Now, she had *me* curious. "Why would you say that?"

Another long pause. Maybe Kelsey was more of a morning person and she needed to think about her words more carefully after ten at night. Or maybe she was deciding if she wanted to share information with me. That was fair. "They've been in the news a lot lately."

Though I suspected there was more she wasn't telling me, I was in no position to press her. "True. I know my sister, Sydney, had a meeting with JB in the late afternoon, early evening on Friday. Her choice of location for the meeting tells me they were trying to avoid being seen."

"Where did they meet?"

"Flying V Campground."

"Interesting choice."

"I suppose. I've never been there and have no idea why they picked such a place. Sydney isn't a big outdoors person."

"Well, that part's obvious. To me, at least."

That made one of us. "Would you like to enlighten me?"

"That depends."

"On?" Though, I was pretty sure I knew where this was going.

"Do you have any other siblings I should know about, identical or otherwise?"

Because there was a slight tease in her voice, it made me feel that maybe I hadn't permanently damaged the trust we'd built. I chuckled a bit. "Sydney is my one and only sister. I am five minutes older. We are identical except for a tiny birthmark she has on the left side of her temple. She blames me, claiming I kicked her in the head so I could be born first. Our parents are Stefano and Delaney Sabatini, and their love for each other grows more perfect with each passing year. Which, I believe, explains why neither Sydney nor I have settled down as we're looking for something in a relationship I'm not sure exists anymore."

That was pretty good sharing, if you asked me. Which, she didn't.

"I'd love to meet them someday."

"I'd love that, too. Next time we have coffee, I'll show you pictures and tell you their story."

"Sounds nice."

There were more pauses in this conversation than the number of times I'd stopped a movie so my younger cousin could go to the bathroom or get a snack when she was little. Finally, Kelsey broke the silence. "Flying V is known to be a place you go to if you don't want to be seen. Usually, people who are engaged in less than legal activities or…"

"Cheating husbands?"

"Why would you jump right to that option?"

"EZ called me out for hanging there with JB. Since I wasn't there, it's a reasonable assumption my sister was."

"EZ was there with Robert?"

"The one and only. Why does that surprise you? I mean, it's no big secret they have something between them."

"True, but normally they aren't seen in public together."

"EZ says no one that Robert cares about would be at the Flying V."

"I suppose, but still…"

I found it ironic that everyone in town, including Robert's wife, Dora Lee, turned a blind eye to the *special* relationship he had with EZ, but appearing in a public place where secret lovers were known to be found was crossing a line. Go figure.

"Look, I have enough on my plate to worry about right now, but curiosity is clawing at me enough to ask the question. Why is it such a big deal? I know you and Dora Lee are somewhat friends or acquaintances, but surely Robert had to know it was a possibility they would be seen. Given his prominence in the community, there might be some nefarious character at the campground who might opt for blackmail. So, why risk it?"

"I've known Dora Lee for a long time, but I wouldn't characterize us as friends. We play nice in the sand box at public functions, but that's about as far as it goes. As a married woman, I suppose I have a bit of sympathy for her in this situation."

"Pete would be an idiot to cheat on you. And before you say it, I know the rumor mill, along with EZ, stand firm that they're just friends, but appearances suggest that while they may not be friends with benefits, there's a special connection between those two. We also know Robert wouldn't do anything overt to upset Dora Lee. I'm sure they have many clandestine meeting places. Why choose one so risky?"

No pause this time, only a long sigh. "I don't know, my friend. I don't know. But I do know that Robert does nothing without a reason. If he was at Flying V with EZ, there was a purpose behind it."

I let that information sink in before I responded, mostly because I had no idea why the esteemed Robert Birmingham would do something so reckless. It wasn't his style. "As much as I would love to brainstorm this mystery with you, I need to focus on family matters."

"I understand. If there's anything I can do to help, you know my number."

"Thanks, Kelsey. And I really am sorry about not telling you about Sydney. I promise to do better in the future."

When she didn't respond right away, I wasn't surprised. One of the reasons I liked her so much was that she didn't speak lightly. Her words had meaning. Because of that, I waited. "I know you've shared more about your past with me than anyone else. I also know you have your reasons, and I do my best to respect them."

"I know," I quickly added. "And I appreciate that very much."

"I just want you to know I'm a trustworthy sort." She chuckled. "Why else do you think I'm the center of the gossip hub? Everyone trusts me to hear them out, and they know whatever information I learn will be treated with respect. And before you make some sassy comment, the only people I ever share any information with is you or Pete, and only if it's relevant to something going on in your life."

"I do appreciate that detail." I smiled even though she couldn't see me. "And I do trust you, more than anyone else around here."

"Then, that's enough for now. Try to get some rest."

"See you tomorrow."

I ended the call and started my nighttime routine. It had been an incredibly long day. Once settled in bed, I took the pad from the nightstand and jotted down notes and questions. It was important to do it now while the details were still fresh in my brain. Sleep fogged the mind and made one forget things they might otherwise remember. At least, that had always been my experience. Exhaling slowly, I started writing:

Sydney's client, CellCo, in the news a lot: possible corporate espionage.

Sydney met with JB Friday evening, Robert and EZ saw them (need possible timeframe).

When did JB get murdered?

Need Sydney to provide her timeline and whereabouts.

Why so quick to arrest? What evidence do they have?

The last question would be the one staying with me as I slept. It was the most pressing of all the information and questions so far–the most pressing one for which I needed an answer. My primary goal: to get my sister out of this mess. If I didn't, not only would Sydney go to jail for a crime she didn't commit, but...

I would have to tell our mother I failed.

Chapter Four

I woke around eight on Sunday morning, tired but relieved by knowing I'd managed some sleep. It was more than I had expected. A quick check of my phone showed missed texts from Jeremy:

Morning, hope you slept well. Fire is 80% contained. Should be out today sometime. Then an investigation will begin. Area is roped off. Rangers, police, and EPA are also on site. We continue to guard the cove and lake to protect boaters. Will call when I can.

With the mention of an investigation, I wondered what he could mean. It was reasonable to assume the cause of the fire, but was there something else? Where had JB's body been found? I hadn't considered it being anywhere near the fire since they'd moved to arrest so quickly. With all the chaos surrounding a forest fire, that seemed unlikely, but I supposed anything was possible.

All those questions would need to wait as Jeremy had other priorities right now. I sent a text in return: *Morning. I'm glad you're safe, though I'm sure you're exhausted. A shower, hot food, and a place to lay your head can be found at my house if you're too tired to drive home. Stay safe!*

I carefully avoided saying my bed was available as I didn't want him to get the wrong idea, not that he would. Better to be cautious and not take any chances, especially when it came to our relationship.

Once that text was done, I took a deep breath and sent one more text. This one was to my mother: *Morning, Mamma. Spoke briefly with Sydney yesterday evening. She's buried with work and upcoming meetings. She promises to call as soon as she's free.*

There. Not technically lies, at least not ones of commission, anyway. Without a doubt, I'd left a lot out. Maybe it would put her mind at ease, at least until I had just cause to worry her.

With that business complete, it was time for caffeine and breakfast. While my cappuccino was brewing, I grabbed a yogurt from the fridge. While a Texas gold bar, one of my favorite treats since moving here, would have been my desired choice, I could hear my mother's voice in the back of my mind reminding me how important it was to fuel your body properly first thing in the morning. As a registered nurse her entire career, I figured she knew a thing or two about health and nutrition. Deciding not to mess with karma (specifically my mother's), I opted to have the gold bar another time.

With my coffee in hand, I peeked outside to see what the sky looked like this morning. Smoke still lingered in the area, but it didn't seem as prevalent as the evening before.

Even if the flames were extinguished today, it would take time for the air to fully be restored to pre-fire breathable levels. I'd just sat down to enjoy my coffee and dive back into the research on CellCo, when my phone buzzed three times in rapid succession. If I remembered correctly, that was a news alert.

The notification read: *Breaking news! Prominent local businessman and board member of CellCo murdered over the weekend. Local woman held for questioning.*

I took small comfort that the names of those involved were not specifically mentioned. Clicking on the article, I read to see what else I could learn.

The body was found late Friday night at Ally's Hangout, a small picnic area situated on the edge of Lake Amore. Though someone has been brought in for questioning, the site still boasts the yellow crime scene tape.

Scanning the rest of the article, I didn't see anything of value. As I wasn't familiar with the location and how it was set up, there was only one way to try to get a better grasp of the situation and JB's last moments. I had to go there. I grabbed my map of Lake Amore and, using a magnifying glass, scoured the shoreline until the small outcropping of land known as Ally's Hangout was located. Using a pencil, I circled the area to easily locate it later. The best way to approach would be on the water to minimize the number of people I might encounter. There was a small strip of land nearby. I could park my kayak on the far side of it and walk from there. Though the kayak wouldn't be fast should I need to get away quickly, it would allow more places to hide on the lake and the ability to get into spots others could not.

I chose my clothes carefully. I wanted to appear somewhere between civilian and civil servant. This was not an official con, but depending on what or who might be there when I arrived, it never hurt to be prepared with a cover story.

Paddling quietly, the kayak was steered to stay as close to the shoreline as possible. The waves were gentler than normal, probably because fewer boats were out. Sunday mornings were typically quieter, but with the fire and part of the lake being protected by the game warden and other law enforcement, it appeared most had decided to forego the lake today.

I kept the bandana around my nose and mouth to minimize the smoke creeping into my lungs. Thankfully, my destination wasn't too far away from the marina. I tied off my kayak and took a deep breath. Pulling a small notebook from my back pocket, I walked with purpose toward Ally's Hangout. Sometimes, merely looking like you belonged somewhere kept people from asking questions, or at least too many.

As the article reported, yellow crime scene tape left no doubt that something horrible had happened here. A few picnic tables were arranged several feet apart and an outdoor grill was cemented into the ground. I could see where this would be a nice place for a family to come on a weekend for a meal and maybe some swimming in the lake.

A middle-aged man with blond, tight curls that were untamed and frizzing in the growing humidity was collecting evidence. He noticed me slipping under the tape. "Hey, hey, who goes there? Can I help you?"

"I certainly hope so. They sent me for an update." It was a shot in the dark, but worth taking. Otherwise, I'd have to leave without getting any information and come back in the dark. I wasn't a fan of that idea. I skipped over his question, no sense volunteering unnecessarily.

"Oh, they did, did they?" He stood and arched his back in a big stretch. "Well, you can tell them I'm working as fast as I can. You might want to remind them they sent one tech... *one* to process this entire crime scene."

I had no idea why they only sent one person or, to be honest, what the normal complement of forensic techs would be at a crime scene. If the television shows were accurate, there would be a couple more people here at least. "I will remind them. I'm sorry you're having to go this alone. Have you learned anything I can share?"

My words tempered his anger and frustration a bit as he sighed. "Fine. Two casings were recovered here." He pointed to an area just past the table closest to the area entrance. "This indicates the shooter would have been standing about here." He walked over to the opposite end of the point nearest the lake. "Based on the info I have, I'm thinking the victim was sitting at the table when they hit him. Given the proximity of the casings, two rapid fire shots to the same area, so the vic wasn't running."

As nervous as JB had been, if someone had come into the area, they would've passed right by where he sat. If it was someone whom he was wary of, no way would he have just sat there and let them shoot him. To me, that meant he knew his killer.

"However, as I'm sure you're aware, this is a public area. We can catalog and process every gum wrapper, popsicle stick, and piece of chewing gum, but it doesn't mean anything unless we happen to have DNA of a suspected killer to match it to."

I was still trying to process what he'd shared about the body and the bullets, so I answered without thinking. "They have a suspect in custody for questioning."

He hobbled over to stand a few feet in front of me. His face turned red, more from anger than the sun. "Are you friggin' kidding me? Why am I still here, then? I know everyone's busy with all the drug stuff, but still…"

"Drug stuff?"

"Yeah, the sheer number of drugs filling our streets and schools. Unless you've been living under a rock, you should know about that. What department are you with?"

Oh, this needed some serious misdirection. "I've heard, but I assumed you meant a recent development. How about we do some mutual sharing of information? I can tell you why I think you haven't been informed about the suspect, and you can give me the latest update on the drugs." It most likely didn't have any relevance to this case, but it might help Emerson and me with our little side investigation, even though it hadn't really started yet. Maybe this would give me some idea *where* to start. My main goal, however, was to refocus his thoughts away from me. My brain wouldn't let me ignore the fact that whatever was going on with these drugs in our county had apparently meant processing a murder scene had taken second fiddle on the priority list.

He sat down heavily at one of the tables. "Sure, why not?"

Whew, dodged a bullet on that one... At least, so far. Wanting to show good faith, I started. "They only took the suspect into custody late last night here at the local office. Chief Parker is holding her until Monday morning when an attorney can be present for her to be questioned. No arrests have been made yet." I was hopeful the last bit would make him feel better about being sent out here by himself.

He pulled a snack bar out of a pocket inside his protective gear. "Sorry, my sugars are dropping."

"Of course, please help yourself."

After a few bites, he exhaled a long breath. "I know I'm cranky. Between the blood sugar issues, being overworked, and–"

"Underpaid," I supplied with a smile.

"Yeah, that, too. I get aggravated. And I got a kid, too, in high school in Waylan County. We live just across the county border. He goes to school there, and I work for this county. He plays football and is pretty darn good."

"Texas high school football, it's big. Sounds like you picked just the place you wanted him to be."

"Yeah, but lately I'm thinking about moving to the country and home schooling him. The missus has a degree in education, ya know."

"Because?"

"Hello?" He graced me with a wide-eyed stare of disbelief. "Kids are dying. It's crazy!"

"From the drugs?" Since that's how this line of conversation started, it was reasonable to assume.

He chuckled, but it sounded more like a hyena who had just escaped a lion's grasp than a sigh of mirth. "Yeah, the drugs. Another young girl died this weekend from an OD. That's where everybody else is, I assume."

"Yes, yes. Though, I hadn't heard about the girl yet." While we were talking, I kept my head on a swivel, trying to see something that might have been missed or some clue as to how they pinned this on Sydney so quickly.

The man stood. "Well, I'm sure it will be on the six o'clock news. And since I don't want them reporting me slacking on my responsibilities, I better get back at it."

"Of course. It looks like you have everything under control and are doing a fine job with limited resources. Just one more question. Where did you find the gun?"

"What?"

"The murder weapon, I presume?"

"I don't know what department sent you, but they are out of the loop or ignoring the reports."

"Probably both," I chuckled, a little nervous that if I supplied a name, he might reach out to confirm my identity while I was here.

His laugh this time resonated as a little more normal. Maybe his blood sugars were leveling out. "No murder weapon's been retrieved at this time. Once they can spare some bodies, they'll probably send divers. I say good luck to them. I ain't getting in that lake. No way and no how. You can tell 'em I said that, too."

"How in the world did they find a suspect so soon, then?"

"Ain't my department, lady. I find the evidence, bag, tag, and process it. Everything other than those details is someone else's problem."

"Fair enough. Thank you, sir, for holding down the fort here as it were."

"Aw heck, no one calls me sir except my kid when I'm fussing at him. Just John is fine."

"Well, Just John, thanks for the update."

I started back the way I came, slipping under the crime tape and taking one final look around. As my head turned away from the crime scene, I noticed a direct line of sight to the marina, but more specifically the area where the houseboats were located. I didn't know who else lived there besides Lester, but it was worth seeing if anyone saw or heard anything late Friday night. Depending on available lighting and shadows from the trees, it's possible someone in the houseboat area might have seen something.

Only one way to find out.

I'd just cleared the area of the park and was heading back to where my kayak was waiting, when Just John–as I decided his name would be going forward–called out, "Hey, I didn't catch your name!"

"Thanks so much for all your help, Just John. Have a great afternoon." I then disappeared around some bushes before race-walking to my kayak. I retrieved my wide-brimmed hat and removed the button-up shirt I had on along with the cargo shorts I'd been wearing. Now, I was simply a woman out on the lake, in my bathing suit, enjoying a nice ride. I'd made it far enough from the shoreline by the time he'd rounded the bend, and because my back was already to him, my hope was he couldn't readily identify me.

The trip to the marina was made in short order. The day was going by too quickly and I wanted to investigate this before meeting with Sydney. I maneuvered my kayak into my boat slip and tied it off. After redressing, I pulled out my phone and dialed the number to the local station. I waited for several rings until a gruff voice answered, "Wilson Sheriff's office."

"Good morning, this is Sadie Sabatini. I'd like to know what time I can visit my sister."

"Later," the man barked. I was pretty sure I recognized who the voice belonged to.

"Could you be more specific, please, Deputy Matthews?"

Murmurings of words that should not be uttered, especially on a Sunday, could be heard from the other end of the connection. My guess was he had put his hand over the phone and lowered it to allow himself to vent the majority of his frustration before taking the rest out on me. "In case you've forgotten, everyone was working last night so now we're taking staggered shifts to get some rest. Chief won't be here until around one. He was clear you weren't to be here without him. Pretty sure it's 'cause he doesn't trust you."

"Or..." I drawled, "Maybe it's *you* he doesn't trust." Given the history of interactions between me and Deputy Matthews, this was probably a wise move on the part of the chief, regardless of his reasons.

"Don't show your face here until one this afternoon. Got it?"

"Got it." And with that not-so-pleasant exchange completed, it was time to get on with my investigation.

Lester Price, the marina manager, was outside his office building (more of a two-room structure housing a desk, monitors for the security feeds, and a storage area) pacing and mumbling under his breath. Though he'd cleaned up his act and the marina quite a bit since his sister, Jackie, got elected to the town board, he still reminded me of what Santa would look like after partying all night with the elves and then falling down a chimney. "Lester? Is everything all right? I need to talk to you."

At the sound of my voice, he stopped pacing and jerked his head in my direction. "What? How? I mean, I'm surprised to see you."

Now that he was facing me, I could better understand why Kelsey thought he'd been in a fight. "Oh my goodness, are you okay? What happened?" Maybe the beating he took made him forget I rented a slip here at the marina.

"Right, right. It's just...ugh! Never mind. Just leave me alone. What happened to me is none of your dang business."

While Lester and I weren't besties by any means, my presence seemed to upset him even more than usual. Despite getting along with most people here in Wilson, Deputy Matthews and Lester didn't belong to that group. With run-ins from both of them, today wasn't my lucky day, I figured. "As much as I'd like to leave you alone, I need to ask you a couple questions."

"Well, I'm not in the mood to be answering any, so move along."

My irritation surfaced, but I knew it wouldn't help the situation. "Look, I'm sure the fire has you concerned, but Jeremy texted me earlier sharing that it's almost contained. Given the distance from the marina, I think you'll be safe." Using a soothing voice, I added, "I know you've worked hard in recent months to make the marina much nicer. It's going to be okay."

He stepped closer. "You have no idea what I'm dealing with. The fire is only one of my problems, not even the biggest one." The scoff in his voice as he finished gave me pause.

Realizing I'd momentarily forgotten his childhood friend had just been murdered, I laid my hand on his arm. "You're right. I'm so sorry about JB. I know you two were friends."

Instead of comfort, his face turned a deeper red, and negative energy oozed from every fiber of his being as he jerked away from my touch. "You know nothing! Now, leave me alone and mind your own business!"

This was aggressive, even for him. Grief manifested itself in many ways. A brusque kind of guy by nature, maybe his pain manifested itself in rage. "Believe me, I want nothing more than to do exactly that. However, I need to talk to you about Friday night."

At the mention of that evening, he stopped pacing and faced me, his expression unreadable. "What about it?"

"I couldn't help but notice your houseboat has a clear line of sight to where JB was murdered. Did you see or hear anything that night?"

The confusion on his face created doubt in my theory that he could have seen anything. After a couple moments, his face turned angry again as he resumed his pacing. "What I saw or didn't see is none of your business. And, apparently, it doesn't matter, anyway."

His statement made no sense. To me, it mattered a whole lot. He was standing in front of me now, a few feet away. Close enough for me to read the expression behind the crankiness he was projecting.

It was fear.

What in the world could inspire this level of anxiety in a man who, up to this point, hadn't seemed to be afraid of anything? I decided to soften my approach. "Look, I have no idea what you're talking about, and believe it or not, my intention was not to upset you when I came here. I'm only looking for information to help my sister." Maybe the fact we both had sisters we were trying to help would cause him to soften.

"You have a sister?"

While I'd wished I'd shared more of my personal life with Kelsey, even if I had decided to be more talkative about such things, it wouldn't have been with Lester. Since I'd opened the door, I might as well continue through it. "Yes, a twin, actually."

Instead of easing his concern, my admission sent him further off the edge. "A twin? You've got to be kidding me." His head started shaking as his pacing and mumbling resumed.

"Identical twin to be exact."

"Un-friggin-believable. This is a nightmare." He whirled on his heel and faced me. "You are a nightmare!"

He lifted the small flask he'd been holding to his mouth. Despite being Sunday, no way were the contents of that container communion wine. After a long draw, his attention was captured by something behind me. I turned to see a man who'd just walked into the marina. He was tall, with coal black hair slicked back and eyes to match. His suit looked strangely out of place at a marina, but since it was Sunday, it's possible he'd come straight from church. He didn't smile and didn't say hello, simply crossed his arms and leaned against one of the buildings. His non-verbal communication spoke volumes to Lester, though. After a look at the man, he turned back to me. "I'm done answering your questions. And if you know what's best, you'll stop sticking that nose where it doesn't belong." With that final warning, he walked over to the man, who then followed him to the houseboat area.

Our conversation was done.

To get in the last word, I muttered to his retreating form, "You didn't actually answer any of my questions." It was that detail that upset me. Not only did I not get any information, he'd left me with more questions than when I started.

Maybe someone else who lived in a houseboat could help. I spotted his sister watching from the door of her shop. Moving closer, I managed a small smile. "Hey, Jackie. So, I guess you heard that fun exchange?" Figured I might gain more ground with his sibling. It wouldn't take much, seeing how I'd made zero progress with him.

She didn't offer a smile in return. Instead, worry lines creased her forehead. "Oh, hi, Sadie. Only a little. I'd apologize for him, but there's not much point, I think."

"Not really, though he seems much worse than normal. Who was that man?"

She looked around nervously before her gaze returned to mine. "His name is Jason Devlyn. Not someone you want attention from."

"Yet, your brother just walked away with him."

She pulled her bottom lip into her mouth, her loose curls moving with the shake of her head. "Sometimes, we don't have choices."

I could've made the argument there's always a choice, perhaps not an easy one, though. Lester didn't strike me as the kind of guy who would make the hard ones. "Any idea what he wants with your brother?"

The worry in her slate gray eyes magnified. "I wish I knew. Since the fire broke out, he's visited Lester several times. And each time, my brother has grown more agitated. I've tried talking to him, but surprise, surprise, he's not interested in sharing."

I could feel my brow furrow as I considered what she said. "I'm not sure why the fire would upset him so much, but my presence certainly irritated him more than usual." I held up my hands in a gesture of surrender. "I know he's not my biggest fan, but this seemed out of character, even for him."

"I truly have no idea."

I believed her. "When did he get in the fight?"

She sighed. "A few days ago."

"No idea with who?"

She shook her head again. "He's a closed book when it comes to me. I thought getting elected and running for another political office might make him respect me more, but that hasn't really worked out."

Though they fought a lot, deep down I think all she really wanted was a big brother she could be proud of, and who would be proud of her in return. The thought of siblings and Sydney's freedom at stake prompted me to try a different angle. "Maybe you can help me. I need to talk to any residents in the houseboat area. Do you know any of them or who might have been here this past weekend?"

She shook her head. "No one that I know of. With the summer being melt-your-face-off hot, a lot of the usuals have stayed north where it's at least a little cooler. I reckon they'll be back come late fall or early winter."

Sighing, I had to admit defeat for the moment. "All right, it was worth a shot." I hesitated a moment before adding, "Look, I know we're both pretty much in the dark when it comes to Lester, but I know you're worried and there was fear in his eyes. You wouldn't know this about me, but I've always had a knack for helping people who find themselves in impossible situations. I'm here to help if either of you need it."

She studied me for several seconds before nodding. "I appreciate that, thank you."

With nothing more to say and my card only granting me access to my part of the marina where my boat was housed,

I returned to my kayak and made my way home. Thoughts of Lester occupied my brain as I smoothly stroked through the water. There had been a change in him the past six to nine months. Not only had he cleaned himself up, but he'd also made a concerted effort to bring the docks back to code. Jeremy had shared his surprise that no fines had been issued for some time, which, for Lester, was unusual. The fact he'd been able to keep his job for so long while performing poorly had been a mystery to many around Wilson. Maybe he'd changed to ensure he didn't derail Jackie's political career? I didn't entirely buy him being selfless as he'd primarily demonstrated he was nothing but self-serving up to that point.

People change, I reminded myself. Sometimes for good, sometimes for evil, but it was a possibility. Which brought me to how he'd reacted to me today. He genuinely seemed surprised to see me. Given I went to the marina often, it didn't make any sense.

Before I rounded the bend that would put the dock at the back of my property in view, I stopped and looked in the distance where the fire was being contained. It was *not* to try for a glimpse of Jeremy as that would be something a hormonal teenager would do. It was odd to see so few boats on the lake, especially in the summer. Lake Amore was not only a favorite amongst residents, but many tourists enjoyed their summer vacations here. Weekends were especially popular. Maybe the heat had kept people away.

Since I couldn't really see anything, I resumed my trek home. This time, my thoughts went back to Just John and his worry over the drugs in his son's school. Drugs were a terrible stain on our society. When it affected our youth, it was even worse. Teens were at such a vulnerable time in their lives to begin with, it made them easy prey for "quick fixes" to escape their troubles. My team and I had occasionally run across drug-related incidents but had always decided taking on a cartel was more than we could reasonably do. Four people against a well-organized and violent establishment was unrealistic. Now, being a team of one, it was out of the question. I had to figure out how to help Emerson, though. Given what I'd learned from Just John, Emerson's fears were justified.

Shaking the feelings of disappointment as I arrived home, I sent a text to Jeremy: *Not sure when you're getting off or how long you'll have, but the offer of a place to shower and rest your head at my house still stands.*

If he accepted, once he was rested, fed, and clean, I'd use the opportunity to fill him in about Sydney. Hopefully, he hadn't received any alerts about an arrest warrant being issued against me. I wanted the chance to get in front of this and explain. Always better to be on the offense rather than defense. Especially with him.

Making my way inside, the thoughts of all the challenges I'd encountered today blanketed me with heavy worry. Exhaling a deep breath, I knew I could (or should) only tackle one problem at a time. And right now, Sydney's issue was priority number one. Feeling the dampness of my clothes thanks to the heat and humidity from my time out on the lake, a shower was in order. Before I could make it to the bathroom, my phone buzzed. It was a text from Emerson. *Ms. Sadie, can I come over? Need to talk.*

I checked my watch. There was still plenty of time before visiting hours started. I typed a quick reply: *Of course, give me 15 minutes. I'm available until 1, then I have an appointment.* No sense in going into details right now. Though, given how plugged in this kid was to everything that happened in our neighborhood, he probably already knew. Maybe that's what he wanted to talk to me about. He was probably upset I hadn't mentioned my twin before, too. Time to face the music.

Emerson was ringing my doorbell one minute after I'd showered and changed. He was now fifteen years old, though his cherub-like face and mop of brown, curly hair made him seem younger than his actual age. He used that to his advantage in a skillful way as people tended to trust that face and smile. They shared things when he was around, whether he asked or not, and he was a very good listener. His knowledge of the town and the people in it had come in handy for me in the past. I smiled and invited him in. "Morning, Emerson. I thought you'd be in church with your auntie this morning."

He stepped inside, his tall frame more graceful than one would expect. "Usually, I am. Today has been tough, so she told me I could come visit you instead."

For his Aunt Isabella to let him skip church to talk with me, it must be serious. "Then let's get some of your favorite sparkling water and you can tell me what's going on."

I retrieved our drinks and gestured for him to sit in the living room. I waited patiently as he took a few sips. He appeared to be gathering his thoughts. After a couple minutes, his dark, watery gaze found mine. "A friend of mine from school OD'd this weekend."

"Oh no, Emerson!" I moved over to sit beside him and put my arm around his shoulders to offer comfort. "I'm so sorry." Everything Just John shared with me flooded to the forefront of my mind again. "I heard this morning that someone had died but had no idea you knew them, or I would've called. I'm so sorry."

His curls moved as his head shook. "You couldn't have known. She...this just happened in the middle of last night."

This must have been a girl he had a special relationship with for him to be one of the first to learn of her death. I squeezed him tighter. "That's terrible news. You must have been very close."

"We were. You have to believe now that we have to do something, Ms. Sadie. This is the third death in my school district in the last six months, all because of drugs." He lifted his head and scooted out of my embrace a little so he could turn to look at me. "It's just so wrong."

Teenage emotions were fragile things, and I needed to tread carefully. "I've never disagreed that something needs to be done, but I'm just unsure what you and I can do. We have to be careful, Emerson. Sadly, people, even younger ones, have been dying from overdoses for a long time now. It's tragic, but unfortunately a part of the world we live in."

He abruptly stood. "I know people die every day for lots of reasons. My parents died for *no* reason, but that's not why I'm so upset."

"There's a reason, we just haven't found the one for your parents yet. But we will, Emerson. I promise. Someday, you and I, we're going to get to the bottom of that."

His expression softened. "I know, and I believe you." He exhaled slowly and stood tall. "What I'm trying to say..." He paused, probably for effect. "...this is more than usual, which tells me something changed."

Emerson had suffered so much loss in his young life, I couldn't find it in myself to disagree. "All right, I trust you and your instincts. If you say something has changed, then it has. I'll look into this matter."

"You have to let me help."

This time, it was my head that shook. "I'm sorry, Emerson. Drugs come from drug dealers who are supplied by drug cartels. Even as gifted as you are at getting information, cartels are a mean and nasty business. Not only would your Aunt Isabella never forgive me if I put you in harm's way, I would never forgive myself. You're my one Italian-loving friend here in Texas." I tried to soften the blow with a smile at my statement, but one look at his face told me my efforts hadn't worked.

"Look, you either tell me what I should be doing or I'm going to figure it out on my own. Your choice."

Ultimatums from a teenager, gotta love that...not. The determination in his gaze and the set of his jaw told me he would not be moved. I either had to involve him or he'd go off on a crusade by himself. "Okay, give me a minute to think."

Apparently satisfied with my answer, he sat down on the sofa and returned to his beverage. I took a few calming breaths to allow strategies to assemble in my brain. Sorting through them one by one, I tried to find something to both appease and keep him safe. The plan also needed to allow me to focus on Sydney's challenges before diving headlong into this drug issue. I'd promised Emerson I would investigate this, and I would. However, priorities had to be assigned to each situation. After several minutes, the beginnings of a plan formed. Sitting down to face him, I ensured my demeanor was one hundred percent serious. "Okay, this is what I need you to do. I want you to work on gathering statistics from the past year on drug-related deaths in our county."

"But–"

"But nothing. We're going to need help to win this battle and get to the bottom of what's going on. The best way to get assistance from the authorities is to show them the numbers and make our case. As good as you and I are, Emerson, we can't take on a cartel by ourselves. We're going to need skilled resources. We get that help by gathering intel."

His eyes rolled and a slight huff escaped, but I didn't let that deter me. "Information wins wars. If I had more time, I'd give you countless examples to support my position. I'm not discounting the boots on the ground efforts, but they are more effective when they know where to strike, right?"

He crossed his arms but answered reluctantly, "Yes, ma'am."

"All right, then. We need to start with learning what we can. We need to know if there's really been an increase in deaths due to drugs or if they're just hitting closer to home for us lately. You can dive into that while I'm dealing with some other matters, and then we will take what you learn and make our battle plan."

"Oh, that's right. Your sister is in trouble. I'm sorry, Ms. Sadie. I was too mad and upset to think about anyone else. I just wanted to talk to you."

"It's okay. Friends help friends when they need it, no matter what's going on in their lives. We'll get through all this together. Deal?" I wasn't even going to ask how he'd learned about my sister. The kid had ways of learning things and always seemed to be right behind Kelsey on the front line of the information scene.

"Yeah..."

I sat up straighter and gazed directly into his dark eyes. "Emerson, this isn't a game. I need you to promise me you'll keep your efforts to research until we can focus on our next steps. Understood?"

"Okay," he sighed. "I promise."

He stood and I followed suit, pulling him into a quick hug. "Please stay safe," I whispered. "I couldn't bear it if anything happened to you."

He squeezed me a bit tighter in response before pulling away with a cheeky grin. "I'm always safe."

I pushed him further away with a smile. "Yeah, yeah, I know. Now, go on. We both have work to do."

He made it all the way to the door before he turned around, his face stoic once again. "If you need help with this thing with your sister, you better text me."

Nodding, I smiled. "I promise."

Once he left, I sent a quick text to one of my former teammates. While I knew Emerson would use every resource available to find the information I'd mentioned, my IT whiz kid, Jessica, could access places Emerson and I could not. Pulling up the app to send an encrypted message, I typed: *J, need info on candy for babes in my store.*

Even with a secure delivery system, we always used code we'd developed over the years. One time when we'd encountered a low-level drug dealer, I'd asked him how he slept at night making his living off dealing poison to the people on the streets. He'd shared it was easier than taking candy from babies. From that point on, anytime we were talking about drugs, that became our reference. The reference of my store meant the county I lived in.

A moment later, she replied: *Will find source and distribution of candy for your store.*

There was a delay, but the three dots on the screen showed me she was still typing. Finally, words appeared on the screen: *Watch your 6. Candy draws the taipan.*

Chapter Five

Her warning was noted, but not needed. The taipan held the esteemed title of being the world's most venomous snake. The message was received loud and clear: tangling with this particular brand of snake could kill me in a matter of moments.

I'd have to worry about that later. Now was the time to worry about getting my sister out of her current jam. I sent a quick reply: *Always*.

A moment later, I decided to ask for one more piece of information. *411 Jason Devlyn or Devlin needed*. I added the second iteration as I wasn't sure of the exact spelling. It was also possible there were multiple ways Jason was spelled, but Jessica was smart and would run all variations.

Checking the clock, I had about an hour before my scheduled visit with Sydney. Wanting to be as prepared as possible, I decided to do some homework before our meeting. Time to learn a little more about CellCo. Denise and Kelsey had offered nuggets of information, but there was always more to learn.

Settling at the laptop, I typed the company name in the search bar. The first result was a link to an interview with one of CellCo's board members. Since JB was also on the board, this was a decent place to start. This interview was done by a local news station. They were interviewing the Chairman of the Board, Scott McIntyre. For some reason, that name rang a few small bells inside my head, but nothing I could pinpoint specifically with all the other madness floating around in there today. I jotted his name down and then clicked on the video.

The man looked to be around the same age as Robert Birmingham. Salt and pepper hair, still mostly pepper. I hardly noticed the lack of facial hair due to his piercing blue eyes. Though he was smiling at the interviewer, the glints of steel in his gaze told a different story. He was not a man to be trifled with. The conversation lasted about ten minutes, with him sharing the merits of a hybrid solution for power needs. He remained adamant that a combination of alternate energy along with the trusted oil and gas was best for the industry, the local economy, and the environment.

Denise had mentioned controversy over their research and dealings in the realm of alternative energy. Typing in a new search regarding that and CellCo, I clicked on the most popular result. There was a lot of scientific jargon I glossed over while sending up a prayer it wasn't relevant to my concerns. CellCo had invested a lot of capital and resources into developing batteries for use in electric vehicles. I scanned further down the article and learned the challenges to implementing these effectively had to do with many factors like power density, durability, and cost. However, the major concerns surrounded stability.

I narrowed my search to learn more about these issues. Cost was significant in that each battery could result in a final price up to one hundred thousand dollars and a high-range electric car would need at least eight hundred of them. That was crazy expensive, even for the upper echelon of Wilson. They were also expensive to develop, which explained CellCo applying for government grants to help defray research costs in switching from lithium-ion batteries to the new solid-state ones. Since my time was limited, I focused on their stability. With the ever-changing development of the battery, the debate over the recycling and/or disposal of them and their long-term effect on the environment was of primary concern. Once Jeremy was safe and rested, maybe he and I could chat about this.

Most of the articles contained different variations of the same information. I did find it interesting that the arguments provided by Scott McIntyre didn't quite mesh up with the data I'd found on the Internet. Maybe CellCo had developed a cost-effective way to create these batteries and, ultimately, dispose of them. Or maybe he was putting a fantastic spin on everything. Sydney might have even helped him. I'd have to ask her about that.

Before closing down my laptop, I created Google alerts for CellCo, JB Nester–along with other iterations of his name; James Robert, Jim Bob, and the list went on–and, for good measure, Scott McIntyre and Jason Devlyn. It never hurt to have new information to consider.

The hands on the clock had moved quickly. It was almost time to visit Sydney. I grabbed some antipasto salad, utensils, napkins, two sparkling waters, and my entire stash of Texas gold bars. I'd need to visit Tessa this week to restock, but desperate times called for the very best of path-smoothing goodwill gestures.

I arrived at the community police building at one. Chief Parker was waiting for me. "I figured you'd arrive exactly at the time we gave you."

"You know how I like to be precise." I couldn't swear to it, but I thought the smallest hint of a smile crept onto his tired face.

"What's in the basket?"

I opened it up to show him the contents, pulling out all but one of the desserts. "Just some lunch for me and my sister, if that's all right? I wasn't sure what the options for her would be in here."

"Well, she refused breakfast," he gruffed. "She's more like you than just in looks."

"Don't take it personally, she's never been much of a breakfast person. The gold bars are for you and your team."

"We can't accept bribes. You know that."

"What on earth would I be bribing you about? You're letting me see my sister, even before you knew about Tessa's treats. I've not asked for anything else, and–" I quickly interjected, "I'm not going to. So, there's no potential for bribery."

He eyed the gooey, sweet treat and finally relented. "All right, I'm sure the team will appreciate having some baked goods. It's been a long twenty-four hours."

I was tempted to tell him the goodies were for everyone but Deputy Matthews, but knew that would erase any goodwill I might be earning myself. "You don't even have to tell them they're from me. You can be the hero."

He frowned. "I'm not going to lie. If they ask, I'll tell them they're courtesy of Ms. Sabatini."

I nodded and inwardly smiled. We'd let them figure out which Ms. Sabatini he was referring to. Maybe I'd tell Sydney to ask them later if they enjoyed the goodies she arranged. That would provide a little amusement in an otherwise serious situation. The chief led me into the office that served as the interview room. The four walls were painted soft beige, and a single painting hung on the one opposite the door. There were no mirrors. They weren't even going to try to create the illusion that someone outside the room may be watching.

A minute later Sydney was escorted in. She looked fairly good for a woman who'd spent the night in our town's version of a jail cell. She saw the table laid out with our lunch and offered me a big smile. "Is this..."

"Nonna's recipe? Yes, it is."

She quickly took her seat and dove right in. "Thank goodness, I'm starving!"

I chuckled. "Why didn't you eat the breakfast they offered?"

She looked up from her plate, a bite of salad still resting on her fork. "Do you know what they brought me?"

"No idea."

"Sausage and grits. Grits!" she repeated in case I hadn't heard her. "Who brings a woman in her thirties a meal consisting of fat, cholesterol, grease, and whatever grits are? No, thank you. I'd rather be hungry."

"I'll ask the chief if I can bring your food in until we get you out of here."

Her rapid blinking made me worry she had something stuck in her eye. "Thanks, sis. I really appreciate the overnight bag, too. The picture..." She drew a deep breath. "This means a lot. I'm sorry to drag you into this mess."

I grabbed her hand, "Hey, we're sisters–twin sisters at that. I think it's an unwritten rule to be there for each other. We're going to get through this. Now, let's eat and then talk about everything. I don't know how long they'll let me stay."

We finished our food in silence, and I split the one gold bar I'd saved. "I love you, but we're sharing dessert."

She took a bite. "Oh, this is delicious," Sydney offered as she licked some of the goo off her fingers.

"When all of this is behind us, I'll introduce you to Tessa Tucker. She owns the sweet shop a few doors down from mine. Her inventory can put you in a sugar coma faster than you can say thank you."

"I can't wait to meet her." Her smile quickly faded. "Hopefully, I get to meet her."

"Hey, let's try to stay positive. Speaking of that..." I pulled out my notebook. "Let's get down to business. I need you to tell me as much as you can. I need to know about CellCo and your dealings with JB. A timeline will be most helpful."

"Why are you helping me? Besides the familial obligation, that is."

"I've spent the last decade or so trying to help people I didn't even know. I'm certainly going to help someone I know and love."

"I thought you retired from whatever exactly it was that you did."

I shrugged. "No better reason to come out of retirement than to help you."

"I guess."

Ah, now that's the sister I remembered. She was always the practical one, the dream killer, and so very matter of fact. I, on the other hand, tried to look past all of that, see the good and possibility in each situation, and right the wrongs when life dealt an unfair hand to someone who couldn't stand up for themselves. "Okay, moving on. Tell me about CellCo. Why was your firm hired?"

Sadie stood and started pacing. I continued to wait. I knew my sister well; pushing her wouldn't get me the information I needed any sooner. "My firm was hired to help CellCo's public image. You've probably seen them getting a lot of press lately."

I nodded. "Yes, and not for anything good."

Sydney chuckled. "There's no such thing as bad press."

"Yet, you were hired."

"Yes, well, too much of a *good* thing can start to be negative."

"I guess," I replied, mimicking her words from earlier. It earned me a quick glare, which I dutifully ignored. "Is there any truth to the corporate espionage claims?"

Her pacing resumed. "Not anything I was officially looped in on."

"But..." The way she made the statement led me to believe there was some unofficial information here.

"I can't."

"Can't what?"

She stopped her back and forth in the small room and met my gaze. "I signed an NDA."

"Are you kidding me right now?"

"I take my promises, both written and verbal, very seriously."

This woman was unbelievable. "Seriously enough to spend the rest of your life in prison for them?"

To her credit, she didn't say anything but graced me with another glare. Gee, this reminded me of our teen years. Finally, I sighed. "Look, let's deal with one problem at a time. I think we both can agree that violating an NDA to your sister comes with less consequences than murder. In case you weren't aware, Texas still has the death penalty for the big stuff. At worst, violating an NDA is a financial penalty or jail time, both of which are significantly less than the payment for murder. Let's tackle the big one first."

"Fine." Sydney stopped pacing and returned to her seat. I took that as a victory.

"Okay." I inwardly breathed a sigh of relief. The Sabatinis were notoriously stubborn. This was a win and I needed to capitalize on it. "Let's start with the biggest question burning in my brain right now."

"Did I do it? Is that what you want to know?" Her crossed arms and irritated tone told me my victory lap was gearing up for reverse.

"No, I know you didn't do it. I want to know how they are so confident that you did."

She sighed. "I honestly don't know."

"Okay, then tell me what you do know."

Her fingers started drumming lightly on the table, a habit she'd had since youth when she was thinking deeply about any topic. "My job was to help reframe their public image and be proactive regarding bad press already out there and what they believed was still to come."

I didn't say anything to interrupt her, just started jotting down notes and nodding my head. "I didn't even know who James was and had no intention of reaching out, but he approached me."

It took me a minute to make the connection, but I wanted to verify. "James, as in James Robert, JB, Nester?"

"Yes. I was surprised he reached out since my main contact was a woman in their marketing department. We answered to the board, though, as it was their decision to bring us in."

"And JB served on the board."

She nodded. "He was very involved in the expansion of that business unit and their development of the batteries. I was introduced to him, along with the rest of the board, earlier in the week and gave them all my business cards in case they had any questions or additional insight to share to help with the campaign."

"When did he initially reach out to you?"

"I think it was Wednesday morning."

"You can't be sure?" Her lack of attention to detail was surprising.

"I'm a little stressed, Sadie, you want to give me a break?" She added crossed legs to her already crossed arms. Why was dealing with family always so much harder than everyone else?

"I'm sorry. I don't mean to be making things difficult. It's just the best way I can help you is to have the clearest picture possible of what went down in the days and hours leading up to JB's untimely death."

"Fine, let me think." She closed her eyes and I waited, silently praying Chief Parker wouldn't end this meeting before I had anything useful to take with me.

"He reached out Tuesday night. We spoke, I took notes, and I asked him to contact me again when he had more information."

"About what?"

"He made some serious allegations against CellCo. I needed more than his words before I could help him."

"What kind of allegations?" This was definitely one thing we had in common. If we didn't want to share information, getting it out of us was harder than pulling teeth. Once I got her to talk with me, I'd tell her to use those same tactics when she was being questioned tomorrow. But, for now, I needed better cooperation. "Sydney, please, I don't know how much time we have left."

"He didn't offer specifics. I think he was scared. He just shared they were up to no good. I told him he would have to give me something more concrete. He called again Wednesday apologizing and said he understood what I needed and would work on getting it. We agreed to meet on Friday evening at the Flying V."

"Any idea why he chose that location?"

She shrugged. "I don't know. I'm not from around here. You tell me."

"I'd not heard of it until a neighbor showed up accusing me of being reckless by being seen in public with a married man at a place where people go when they don't want to be seen together."

The blush covering her face was slightly adorable. "I had no idea."

"You couldn't have. I live here and I'd never even heard of it before Friday night."

"Guess that means you haven't been chasing any married men," she teased. "Though, I'm guessing whichever neighbor showed up at your door tossing accusations your way exhibited a bit of the pot calling the kettle black."

I smiled at her reference. "The only man I've even slightly been interested in is as single as I am. And we don't have time during this visit for me to go into the nature of my neighbor's relationship. Heck, I'm not even sure I understand it."

"Once this is over, I want to hear everything."

I opted not to point out that I would have been happy to share with her at any point if she'd let me know she was in town, or anytime during the past year that I'd been living here. Communication with each other obviously hadn't been a priority for either of us. Instead, I smiled. "Deal. Now, please, let's get back to the details and timeline."

"Okay," she sighed. "We met at the campground. He was really nervous, though. Kept looking over his shoulder and checking his surroundings. It was almost like he sensed he was being followed or watched."

"Did you see anyone?"

"No one who looked suspicious. Just other men and women milling around or sitting at the picnic tables like we were."

"Anyone he recognized?" Sydney wasn't from around here, but JB would have recognized someone out of place.

"Not that he said."

There was no doubt in my mind if he had seen EZ and Robert, he would have recognized them. Albeit for different reasons, it's not like they were low-profile people in the community. "Okay, go on. Did he have proof of corporate espionage?"

Sydney exhaled slowly. "He didn't mention anything about that to me. Though, given what I've learned about the company in the short time I've been privy to information about them, I wouldn't be surprised."

"Then, what was he so worked up about? I get that allegations are bad, but companies face that kind of stuff every day. You were the one who told me there's no such thing as bad press."

"Depends on how bad it is. What he shared with me next was bad, Sadie. Really bad."

It took everything I had not to yell. Instead, I took a deep breath and exhaled slowly. "What was it?"

A knock on the door interrupted our progress. "Time's up."

"Five more minutes, please?" I really needed more information.

There was a long pause. I was thankful it was Chief Parker on the other side of the door. No doubt Deputy Matthews would have denied my request right off the bat. Though the chief was a by-the-rules kind of guy, he also had a heart. "Five minutes, not one second more."

"Thank you!" I turned to Sydney. "Out with it now. No time to waste." I refrained from pointing out how much time we'd wasted already.

She leaned forward and I did the same. "He said he had proof they were improperly disposing of the failed batteries they were developing."

For once, my sister didn't exaggerate the danger. "The solid-state batteries they were developing? Did he give you the proof?"

She shrugged. "He just said batteries. He claimed it was too dangerous and he would show me the proof later."

I sat back in my chair. "And then, he was murdered later that night."

She mimicked my action. "Yes. It had to be sometime after nine as that was the last time I saw him."

This caught my attention. "You met later Friday night, after The Flying V?"

She nodded. "Yes, we agreed to meet up around eight. He said he would provide proof."

"Did you get it?" This was worse than a suspense movie with dramatic music building in the background as the ticking of a grandfather clock marked the time left in our few minutes remaining.

She shook her head as moisture gathered in her dark brown eyes. "No, he said there were too many eyes around and that we would try again later that night. He told me to rent a boat, then lay low. He would reach out with details on when and where to meet him."

"But he never did."

The head shaking continued as tears began to spill. "No, and the last words I ever said to him were that he was being paranoid. Do you know what he said to me in return?"

This time, I mimicked the shaking as words felt inadequate. Instead, I took her hands and squeezed them tightly in support.

"He said–" she drew in a stuttered breath, "–better paranoid than dead."

The blood in my veins chilled at her words. Not only had he been right, but given the timing of everything, he had to have been killed a short time later. "Where were the two of you when you had this final conversation?"

"What? Why does that matter?"

"Because, Sydney, the location could give us some indication as to where he was going to take you to show you the proof."

She wiped her eyes. "Yes. Yes, that makes sense. We were at the lighthouse."

My gaze snapped to hers. "The lighthouse on Lake Amore?"

"Yes, why?"

The gears in my brain were shifting at a rapid pace as I tried to sort out all the thoughts vying for attention. "Because Sydney, that means there's a good chance they disposed of the batteries in the lake. And that–"

"Is very, very bad news," she finished.

Chapter Six

We had no further time to deliberate as Chief Parker knocked again and opened the door. "Sorry, ladies. Time's up."

I nodded. "Thank you for the few extra minutes."

"Of course."

"Can I see her again before tomorrow?"

"Only one visit per day, sorry. But you can call the number here at the station this evening and I'll let you speak on the phone for a bit."

Whether it was the gold bars or he had a soft spot in his heart for sisters, it didn't matter. I was just grateful he was open to letting us communicate. "Thank you. I appreciate it and you."

He nodded and turned to my sister. "Come on, let's get you settled."

"Talk to you later, Sadie."

"Later, Sydney. Love you."

"Love you, too."

I took the long way home, turning down each side street and following it to the eventual cul-de-sac that ended most branches off the one and only road in and out of Wilson. I'd found this to offer both positives and negatives when one was plotting escape plans. I tried to clear my mind of all the noise and focus on the wooded lots, the beautiful landscaping, and the deer that wandered about our little slice of heaven.

The extra time did the trick and recentered my thoughts. I had formulated a plan for what I needed to do next to help Sydney. Of course, all of that took a back seat in my brain when I saw Jeremy sitting on the steps leading up to my front door. He was covered in ash, so the white from his teeth as he smiled shone even brighter than normal. The simple act made me forget all the pressing issues for just a moment as the joy in my heart from seeing him alive and unharmed took precedence. "Hey you. Looks like you could use a shower and a hot meal."

He laughed. "In that order, yes, ma'am."

I used the app on my phone to open the garage door. "Come on inside and we'll get you taken care of. While you shower, I'll make some lunch."

"Lunch, breakfast, dinner—as long as it's a hot meal, I'm ready."

"I can do that. You have a change of clothes?" Though him walking around my house in nothing but a towel would be a vast improvement in the landscape of my life over the last twenty-four hours or so, we hadn't even gone out on an official date yet. So, those thoughts would need to just climb back into my fantasy locker for future use.

He reached behind him and produced a duffel bag. "A boy scout is always prepared."

"Of course you are," I laughed. "Come on, let's get you cleaned and fed, and then you can fill me in on your adventures." That also meant I'd need to fill him in on things as well, especially the potential there could be faulty batteries somewhere in the twenty-plus thousand acres that Lake Amore spanned. Though, I hoped with the information I'd learned from Sydney, we could narrow it down somewhat. The detail she'd shared about JB asking her to rent a boat also meant they could be anywhere. At least he'd have a place to start.

I got Jeremy settled in the guest bathroom with all the necessities and set about making brunch for the hero that he was. Pancakes, turkey sausage (he was probably more of a pork sausage guy, but this girl tried to minimize the fat and calories wherever she could, so that's what was in the fridge), scrambled eggs with cheese, coffee, and juice.

"That smells amazing."

I turned to see Jeremy arrive in the kitchen with gym shorts, a T-shirt, and damp hair. I stopped and admired, just for a moment, how amazing he truly was. Not only was he a fine-looking gentleman, he was also the kind of person I loved having in my life. He helped me become a better person, even if I fought him every step of the way.

"Sadie? Everything okay?"

It wasn't, but in this moment the answer was, "Just a typical Sunday. Come on, a feast fit for a game warden is ready."

He eyed the spread with appreciation. "This looks amazing. Thank you." He stepped closer and placed a chaste kiss on my cheek. Not exactly the level of gratitude I was hoping for, but given he'd been up for God knows how long, I would cut him some slack.

While he ate, I made myself a cappuccino and nibbled on a piece of toast with some hazelnut spread. I didn't partake in this very often, but I felt I'd earned it today. We ate in companionable silence. It felt right.

Once he'd finished, he sat back and put his hands on his six-pack abs. "Thank you so much. That hit the spot."

"It was my pleasure. Thank you for letting me do this for you."

He sat up straighter and reached across the table, taking my hand. He squeezed gently. "Now, will you tell me what's going on in that beautiful head of yours? Something is bothering you."

I scrunched up my face. "What makes you think that?"

"You're never this quiet," he chuckled. "And I can see something's troubling you in those beautiful chocolate drop eyes."

The man could read me like a book, which was dangerous. But in this instance, there was no sense denying it. I needed to tell him things. "Let's grab another cup of coffee and move to the couch where it's more comfortable."

"Normally, I'd worry too much caffeine would keep me from sleeping, but I don't think that's going to be a problem today."

"You want to nap first? My problems can wait."

He pulled me into an embrace. "Sleep can wait. Tell me what's going on. If you don't, I won't be able to sleep from worrying about you, anyway."

I stayed in the comfort of his hug for a few moments more before taking his hand and leading him to sit next to me on the couch. "I'll keep this as brief as possible as I really do want you to get some rest."

He turned on the couch so he could look at me. "Whatever it is, you can tell me."

Hopefully, he felt that way by the time I was finished. I was certain the nap he wanted wasn't going to happen once he learned all these details. I gave him the high-level version of the events leading up to my visit with Sydney just before I came home. He was listening with intent and had taken my hand to offer comfort. Finally, we came to the moment I knew would spark him into action and end our little escape on a Sunday afternoon. "Right before I left Sydney, she told me that JB had proof he wanted to show her that CellCo improperly disposed of batteries. I don't know what kind, but it's reasonable to assume they were failed solid-state batteries they've been trying to develop."

"I'm sorry about your sister and want to circle around to that again, but first, I need to understand why they wouldn't just follow proper procedures? It's not easy, but it's not *that* hard. Heck, they could've called us, and we would've handled it for them."

"Is that in your job purview?"

"In a roundabout way, it could be. Depends on where you tell me they disposed of them."

This was the hard part. "I can't say for sure, but we have a theory." He squeezed my hand in encouragement, and I took a deep breath. "They met at the lighthouse at Lake Amore. He told her to rent a boat and he would provide her details of when and where to meet him. He was paranoid, justifiably so. Said there were too many eyes. We suspect they must have dumped them in the lake somewhere and that's where he was going to take her when they met up again."

Jeremy stood, bringing me with him. "Probably should have led with that. This is bad, Sadie."

"We don't know for sure," I stated, defending myself the tiniest of bits. "It's just a theory, but I felt like you should know."

He gave me a quick hug. "Fair enough. I appreciate your telling me. I need to make some calls."

As I'd suspected, the promise of a nap had been abandoned by my theory, but I would've felt worse if more precious time had been lost if I hadn't shared at all. Telling him first, as he implied, would've been the safest, but even if he could manage on little to no rest, the man needed food to make good solid decisions and think rationally.

When he stepped away to make his calls, I made my way to the kitchen to clean up. The clock on the wall taunted me. It was only late afternoon, however, my internal clock argued the clock simply had to be wrong and that bedtime was just around the corner. I really hated it when my body made that kind of mistake.

Once the dishes were finished, I made another coffee, indulging in an extra shot of espresso. Though a nap would be ideal, with all the things needing to be done, Jeremy and I would both have to forego that luxury today.

I'd made it halfway through my coffee and notes when Jeremy walked back in the room. "Thank you so much for the shower and brunch. I'm going to need to take a raincheck on the nap, though."

"I figured as much. Sorry."

"Don't apologize. Your information will help us hopefully locate and minimize the damage CellCo allegedly has caused. They're keeping restrictions on the lake to allow for essential personnel only until we can complete testing on the water."

I loved that he added allegedly, even though I was pretty sure JB wouldn't have risked his life over an *alleged* incident. "Sounds like a good plan. You'll keep me posted?"

"As much as I can, promise."

I smiled. It was more than I expected, truthfully. Jeremy was as much, if not more, by the book as Chief Parker. He set his backpack down and moved to my position on the couch, reaching out his hand to clasp mine. Pulling me to a standing position, we hugged. It offered a sense of contentment that I was coming to like entirely too much. "I haven't forgotten about your sister. We'll figure it out. You'll let me know if there's anything I can do to help?"

There was, but this didn't feel like the right time to ask. Shaking my head, I smiled. "You have enough on your plate."

"Hey, that's not how relationships work. At least, not relationships with me."

My mouth quirked to the side. "Are we in a relationship?"

The blush suffusing his tanned features was enjoyable and more adorable than he would want me to tell him about. "Enough of one that I care about what happens to you and the people you care about. I'm certain we can have more of a relationship if only we could find time to, I don't know, go to dinner, enjoy boat rides, long walks...you get the picture."

"It's a picture I'm definitely interested in acquiring. Maybe once things settle down?" It was optimism at its finest.

"It's a date." He planted a gentle kiss on my forehead, missing my desired target by about six inches. However, one took what one could get.

"In the meantime, if there's anything I can do, let me know."

"There is one thing..." I hedged. I hated to ask, but the question had been burning in my brain since they showed up to arrest me and took Sydney away instead.

"Name it."

"I can't figure out how they managed to secure evidence, ID me, get an arrest warrant, and show up to execute it in such a short time. You and I both know the wheels of justice don't typically turn that fast here. I mean, JB was a prominent figure, but he's no Birmingham."

"Sadie," he exhaled in a mild warning.

"Sorry, but you know what I mean."

"I do. Let me see what I can find out. No promises, though."

Pulling him into a hug, I added, "Your word is more than enough for me. Anything you can find out will be greatly appreciated."

This time, I did receive a gentle kiss on the lips. A Jeremy kind of promise, sealed with a kiss. I'd take that any day of the week. "Be safe out there. The offer of the spare bedroom still stands if you need it."

"I might take you up on that. The drive back to my house feels entirely too far away at the moment."

The temptation to tease him that my bed was his bed was strong, but truthfully, we'd both be too tired to enjoy either the tease or the implication, so I let it slide. "I'll leave a spare key hidden under the planter next to the back sliding glass door in case I'm not home."

"Thanks. You stay safe, too. I know how you like to get yourself in trouble with your investigations. With everything happening with your sister, can you try to let the authorities handle this?"

I could try, but I wouldn't succeed. "No promises," I smirked, echoing his words. "I will be careful, though. That is a promise."

He sighed. "I guess that will have to do. I appreciate your honesty."

Jeremy left, and I returned to my now cold coffee and notes. I read everything I'd written:

Sydney's client, CellCo, in the news a lot: possible corporate espionage.

Sydney met with JB Friday evening, Robert and EZ saw them (need possible timeframe).

When did JB get murdered?

Need Sydney to provide her timeline and whereabouts.

Why so quick to arrest? What evidence do they have?

PMS hired to deal with bad press.

JB alleged improper disposal of solid-state batteries.

JB believed he was being followed.

Sydney/me believed to be the killer–why?

Last time Sydney saw JB alive was at lighthouse Friday night.

JB killed with 2 shots at Ally's Hangout. Line of sight to houseboats.

Lester acting weirder than normal. Knows Jason Devlyn. Who is he?

Emerson supports Just John's claim of increase in drug-related deaths.

I had no idea if all these things had anything to do with the other, but as they were all loose strands floating about in my head, I thought it best to document them. They could always be discarded later. Given that premise, I decided to add one more thought:

Robert and EZ were at Flying V Campground Friday evening – why?

There was no way that thought had anything to do with the rest of them, but the question had been burning a hole in my head since Kelsey and I spoke about it.

After looking at my notes for a bit, I decided action was needed. Though the lake was technically off limits, I could access the Lake Amore lighthouse from land. I wanted to go look around and see if I could find anything.

Thirty minutes later, I got out of my truck and stared at the swarm of uniformed individuals and every color of lights ever seen on an emergency vehicle blocking my path to the lighthouse. If there was any evidence there, they would either find it or destroy it. While my focus was going to be on JB's murder and the evidence surrounding it, Jeremy had taken the information I shared and ran with it. I saw a lot of jackets with embroidered acronyms that contained everything from EPA to CSD and some I had no idea what they meant. Most likely something to do with the environment. The hunt for the batteries was on. I wasn't sure why the Crockett County sheriff's department was here other than to keep folks like me out. In the distance, I saw more people continuing the work around the fire containment area. The investigation into that still had to be done as well. All our civil servants were having a very busy weekend.

Since the lighthouse was not an option, the next steps to help Sydney were not apparent. I'd already checked out the murder scene. Until I knew more about the circumstances surrounding her arrest or my attorney got her released, I would have to trust the authorities to handle things. For the official record, I was not a fan of this plan of inaction.

"You checking up on me again?"

I switched my gaze from the mass of people to the one standing beside me. "Just John." I smiled and prayed he wouldn't call someone over to arrest me. "They pull you away from the other site to assist on this one?"

"Nah, I finished up there, at least as much as can be done today. Lab needs to run everything and then I'll do a final sweep, probably tomorrow."

Nodding, I waited to see what happened next.

After a few moments, he leaned closer. "You lied to me."

His voice didn't sound angry, not even the frustrated angst from earlier. No, this was more matter of fact. "Technically, I didn't."

He chuckled. "Is that so?"

I faced him with a smile, "It is, indeed. Not once did I identify myself as any branch of law enforcement or other official department. I merely said *they* were looking for an update, and you inferred the rest."

"I..." He stopped and chuckled. "Okay, fine, you're right. You took advantage of my frazzled state."

My mirth faded. "You're right. I did. I'm sorry. I was just trying to learn something to help my sister."

I could see the gears turning as he recalled our conversation. "Is your sister the one they have in custody?"

At this point, I figured there was no reason not to be transparent with him. "Yes. They showed up late Saturday evening with an arrest warrant. She was with him on Friday, but the last place she saw him was here." I pointed to the lighthouse. "Less than twenty-four hours later, he's dead and she's taken in for questioning. And you don't even have the gun. Does that add up to you?"

Just John pulled a snack bar out of his jacket and took a couple bites. "Because you were kind to me, even though you were being deceptive at the time, I'm going to see what I can find out. I have theories, but I'm a man of science so while I trust my gut..."

"Trust, but verify, right?"

He offered a broad grin. "Always."

"I appreciate your willingness to look into this for me."

He waved off my gratitude. "Just give me your number and I'll call once I have details."

Thankfully, I'd committed my burner phone number to memory. I liked Just John, but giving him my phone number felt like a little too much sharing for the second time we met. Though he hadn't asked for my name this time, he probably thought with my number, he would be able to learn all of that on his own. He was an investigator, after all. He liked the thrill of the chase.

"Okay, I'll call or text once I know something."

"Thanks, Just John." I grinned, and he blushed.

"You're not gonna let me live that down, are you?"

"It has a nice ring to it."

"What kind of ring does your name have?"

Even though I believed him when he said he wasn't going to turn me in, depending on the situation, he might not have a choice. "Let's say Sadie." The burner phone was registered to a Sadie Sebastian, so I felt comfortable giving him that much.

"Okay, Say Sadie." He grinned. "If you will stay out of the official investigation, I'll see what I can find out for you."

"Deal." But if I needed to insert myself into the *official* investigation, that's what I would do. On the other hand, having someone who was at least law enforcement adjacent on the inside was always good to have in one's arsenal. I thought Just John could be that guy for me. "Before I go..." I hedged, testing the waters to see if he was open to a little more conversation and fact-finding on my part.

He chuckled. "Yes?"

"One of my younger friends mentioned his good friend OD'd in the early hours of the morning. Was her death the one you mentioned when we spoke before?"

The smile he'd been sporting faded. "Yes, my colleague told me his investigation so far had revealed she'd been at a party. At her young age, I'm thinking she probably was experimenting or someone snuck it in her drink. Tox screens aren't complete yet, of course, but I wouldn't be surprised if it was the same strain we've been seeing. One player is behind all of this. I know it in my gut, and science has supported my theory so far."

"Any progress on identifying the dealer?"

He shrugged. "Sorry, my lane is obtaining, identifying, and documenting the evidence. Other guys take that information and make the magic happen."

The way he said it, I couldn't be sure if he was proud of his role or bitter that his department didn't get more credit. "Without you, the other guys wouldn't know who to go after."

He nodded. "We all have to work together." He finished the last bite of his bar. "Speaking of that..."

"Yes, thank you for your time. I'll let you get back."

"I'm sorry about your friend. I hope we can figure out who's dealing this brand of poison. Drug addiction is bad enough, but being sold dirty drugs makes it even worse. No chance for these kids."

"I appreciate that. If there's anything I can do to help..." There wasn't anything he'd let me do, but I felt compelled to offer.

"Just keep your eyes and ears open, and report whatever you find to the proper authorities."

I grinned as I'm sure that was written in a handbook somewhere about how to deal with well-meaning, but nosey, citizens. "Will do."

I watched the scene for a few more minutes to look for Jeremy, but he must have been back on his boat, patrolling the lake again. Safety was his number one priority. With a wave goodbye to Just John, I returned to my truck.

On the drive home, I decided to stop by Isabella's house and check on her and Emerson. Their one-story brick home sat on one of the aforementioned cul-de-sacs off the main road. The varying shades of gray and charcoal stone provided the perfect backdrop for the splashes of color from the flowers

Isabella had planted in the beds in front of her home. It was obvious that flowers were not only her way of making a living, but a true passion of hers.

I rang the doorbell and waited. A few minutes later, she opened the door, still dressed in her Sunday finest. "Good afternoon, Sadie. Please, come in. Can I get you some sweet tea?"

That particular beverage was a southern specialty. Though I didn't normally avail myself of the sugary drink, the stifling heat gave it extra appeal. "That sounds wonderful, thank you."

She poured the drinks, and we sat at the kitchen table. "You look very nice," I shared after several sips.

"We had a potluck at church today, so I've only been home a short time. Normally, I'd be in yoga pants and a T-shirt by now."

"Comfort clothes at their finest," I laughed. "I can wait if you'd like to change. I really only stopped by to say hello and check on Emerson."

At her nephew's name, her expression sobered. "Thank you for speaking with him this morning. He was very upset. I comforted him as best I could, but I haven't seen him this bad since…"

"Since his parents' untimely death."

"Yes. So, when he asked if he could go speak with you, I couldn't say no. I hope it wasn't an imposition."

I shook my head. "Of course not. Emerson is a dear friend of mine, as are you," I added with a smile. "He's very mature for his age and I think maybe he likes talking to me because I might remind him somewhat of his parents."

"Yes, he enjoys spending time with you. He likes that you give him assignments and take him seriously."

I nodded but decided to hold off saying anything as she seemed to be working up to something. After another moment, she continued. "I appreciate your giving him something to focus on with this whole nightmare with his friend. He wouldn't admit it to me, but I think he liked her as more than a friend."

"I think so, too. Do you have any idea why she was taking drugs?"

"That's the really sad part. From what Emerson has told me, she didn't do drugs. She was at a party and either decided to experiment or someone slipped it in her drink. We don't have the toxicology report yet, but I'm guessing whatever it was must have been laced with something that ultimately caused her death."

Sadness filled my heart with her explanation. I was also impressed that her interpretation of the situation matched Just John's so closely. Kids experimented, they submitted to peer pressure, and they tried things they wouldn't normally do. Someone had taken advantage of that, one way or the other. "That's terrible."

"Yes." Isabella nodded before sipping some more of her tea. "I'm worried about Emerson."

"He doesn't strike me as the kind of kid who would go to a party or submit to peer pressure."

"He's not," she confirmed before the emerald jade of her gaze settled directly on me. "But he is the kind of kid who believes justice should be done. "I know you would never knowingly put him in harm's way, but I'm afraid he may not stop when he should."

"I can't promise he won't, but I do swear to you that I'll do everything in my power to keep him safe. Believe me when I tell you, I've already issued serious warnings to him about stepping outside of the task I've given him."

"Then, let's hope that's enough," she sighed. I couldn't blame her. I worried about him, too, especially in a situation like this. I was sure his aunt's concern was at least ten times more.

"Between the two of us, we should be able to keep an eye on him."

She nodded again, but there was no conviction in her body language to back it up. Wanting to comfort her, I added, "I have a friend looking into all this as well. If she can give me enough information, we can involve the authorities and keep both Emerson and I out of the fray of bringing down these drug dealers."

"Thank you, Sadie. I appreciate all you do for Emerson."

"It's nothing." I waved my hand in dismissal. "Like I said, I enjoy his company and he's a great kid."

"He is," she smiled. "His parents would be proud."

"I have no doubts."

"Speaking of family, how's your sister holding up?"

I didn't really want to talk about her now, but opting for distance right after we'd shared a moment didn't sit right, either. "She's doing okay. I've got a message into my attorney so he can represent her during the questioning tomorrow."

"How did she know JB?"

"Until a few days ago, I don't think she did. Her client was CellCo, and JB reached out to her." I left out anything else as I wasn't sure what was public knowledge versus privileged NDA related information I'd convinced Sydney to provide.

At the mention of CellCo, Isabella's attention snapped to me. "Your sister works for *that* company?"

Her voice trembled a bit as she asked, so I answered without hesitation to clarify. "No, she works for a public relations firm whom CellCo hired to help with their public image. Their name obviously upset you. Do you know something I should be aware of?"

She chewed on her bottom lip for a moment as she studied the pattern of her dress with great interest. Finally, she exhaled slowly and returned her gaze to mine. "Emerson's parents, Edgar and Elena, were investigative reporters. The last story they were working on centered around CellCo. Due to their death, the story never saw the light of day."

While it was slightly suspicious, it wasn't surprising a newspaper or magazine might drop a story that hadn't been fully vetted and written yet. "I'm sure that was very disappointing," I offered in sympathy.

"You don't understand." Isabella stood and began to pace back and forth in the room.

"Don't understand what?"

She paced a few more times before stopping, a haunted expression on her face. "The only reason it wasn't published is because all of their research and notes were never found after their death."

Chapter Seven

Her admission left me speechless for several moments. Finally, I managed, "I had no idea. Even with that detail, they still believed everything was an accident?"

Isabella shrugged. "All evidence pointed to a terrible tragedy. Missing notes and research do not a motive for murder make."

Her tone and demeanor made me believe she'd argued the logic of it being exactly that, but the authorities had not bought it. "Do you know what they were investigating?"

She shook her head. "No. They always kept everything quiet so as not to accidentally leak anything another newspaper could pick up."

"I suppose that makes sense. I've promised Emerson we're going to look into his parents' death. As soon as the current crises pass, I'll dig deeper."

"I'm not sure that's a good idea," she replied as she took our glasses and made her way to the kitchen. I wasn't sure if she expected me to follow or if this was her way of saying the conversation was ending. I opted to wait in the living room.

Once she returned, I had to ask the question. "Why isn't it a good idea?" I was going to need a very good reason to not keep my promise to her nephew.

"Emerson needs to accept their deaths and move forward with his life. Even if we learn it was foul play, it won't bring them back." Tears glistened and my heart hurt at the impossible situation both she and Emerson were in. Closure was important, but I also understood the need to move on. While Isabella may possess the necessary emotional maturity to put all of this behind her, I wasn't sure Emerson was ready or could do that just yet.

I pulled her into a quick hug. "I understand what you're saying, nothing will bring them back. But as Emerson always reminds me about the truth..."

She chuckled. "It will set us free."

"Exactly. We'll figure this out together. I won't do anything without your approval and, if need be, I will explain to Emerson why it might be better to move on and focus on going forward."

Wiping her eyes, she smiled. "You and I both know he will never go for that, but I appreciate your saying the words. Let's talk about it again after things with your sister settle down."

"All right, and thank you for the tea."

I made my way home as I had no other ideas on how to help Sydney just yet. More information was needed, I just had no clue where to go from here. Once back at home, the weight of everything made my eyelids heavy and, seated in my recliner, I gave into the exhaustion and let sleep offer some much needed rest.

The feeling of being watched startled me from my sleep. Cracking one eye open, I saw Jeremy sitting across from me looking worse for the wear. Immediately, I lowered my legs and sat up straight. "What's wrong? Why didn't you wake me?"

"You needed your rest."

My head shook as I dismissed his concern. "So do you, but I'm guessing you haven't had any yet."

"I will, but I needed to talk to you first."

"Then, you should have woken me up." While I appreciated his intent, I was aggravated at myself more than him that I'd slept so long and so deeply. I hadn't heard the camera notification or him opening the front door.

"They found the batteries. At least, some of them. I have no idea if there are more."

This made me forget everything else. "Were they by the lighthouse or in the lake near there?"

His head shook. "No. The personnel investigating the forest fire found them."

Instinctively, my hand went to cover my mouth as the realization hit me. The research had warned of the dangers of improper disposal. And, no big surprise given what I'd been learning about CellCo, they hadn't followed the guidelines. With my mind still hazy from sleep, I didn't think I'd fully comprehended what he was trying to tell me, other than the obvious. "What happened? Besides CellCo not doing what they should with them, I mean. Did they spontaneously combust or something?" Given these were supposed to go inside cars, that felt like a very dangerous proposition.

"It's too early to tell, but based on the talk I overheard, these must have been experimental prototypes or earlier versions with serious flaws. With the high heat and no rain or moisture to offset that heat, the combination must have caused them to spark or somehow reach an internal temperature, which ignited the fire. That's my guess, anyway."

"Wow..." It was an inadequate response to the entire situation, but it was all I had.

"Pretty much."

"You need a shower, food, and some rest...in that order. Then, we can talk more."

"I..." he started, but I stood and pointed to the back of the house where the guest bathroom was located.

"Please, Jeremy. You let me sleep, now I need to insist on some self-care for you."

Grabbing his bag, he stood and headed in the general direction. "Okay, but I do so under protest."

Despite all the bad news from the past twenty-four hours or so, I offered a small smile. "Noted. Now, go. I'll make you a late dinner."

Once Jeremy was gone, I grabbed my phone and headed to the kitchen to see what I could rustle up for food. I had a missed call from the sheriff's office, two missed calls and a text from my mother, and a call from an unknown number. I must have been dead to the world to sleep through all that. As I pulled together the makings of a meal, I video-called my mother.

"Sadie, your father and I have been worried sick. Are you all right? Did something happen?"

The anxiety clearly displayed on my mother's normally calm face brought my guilt for the nap even higher. "Sorry, Mamma, I fell asleep and must have been exhausted as I didn't hear my phone."

She visibly exhaled a sigh of relief. "I swear, you girls are going to be the death of me."

"I really am sorry. I promise it's not our intent to worry you." I wanted to avoid the topic of my sister any more than necessary. I didn't want to even attempt to lie to my mother, especially not when she could see my face. I decided to redirect the conversation. "We had a terrible fire here over the last day or so. It broke out in the forest surrounding the lake."

"Oh no, is everyone okay?"

I nodded. *Except for the man your other daughter is accused of killing.* But mentioning that would be the opposite of what I was trying to accomplish with this topic. "I haven't heard of any related deaths." It was totally the truth.

"That is good news. Do they know what caused it?"

"Besides the heat and drought?"

She chuckled. "Yes, I guess that is a significant factor."

As my mother went on to share about what was going on in their lives over the past few days, I breathed a small sigh of relief that we'd hopefully moved on from dangerous subjects. I continued to prep the food for a late dinner for Jeremy and myself.

"What's for dinner?" My father asked as he joined my mother in the video frame.

"Hopefully, some of her amazing comfort food." Jeremy's voice entered the conversation as he stepped into the kitchen. The phone was immediately grabbed from my father and my mother's wide eyes and grin filled the screen. "Who is this, Sadie?"

The blush on my face had to be crimson red. From the grin on Jeremy's, he'd known exactly what he was doing. I cut him a quick look but couldn't keep the smile off my face, either. "Mamma, Papà, this is my friend, Jeremy. He's a game warden for Crockett County."

I wasn't sure I'd ever seen my mother smile quite so big. "Well, hello, Jeremy. We're Sadie's parents, Delaney and Stefano. It's a pleasure to finally meet you."

"Pleasure's all mine, ma'am. I can see where Sadie gets her striking beauty from."

Oh, he was pouring it on thick, and I loved every minute of it. I couldn't swear to it, but I was pretty sure my mother was also now blushing. "Thank you."

"I couldn't agree more," my father interjected. "We didn't realize Sadie had guests this evening."

Before my father could even get started on whatever road he was about to go down, I made sure both mine and Jeremy's face could be seen as I answered, "I'm providing safe haven to Jeremy, just like Mamma taught me. He's been protecting the lake during the fire and hasn't had sleep in a couple days. I've offered my guest room and amenities to him until he's rested enough that it's safe for him to drive home."

I swear, I could see the disappointment on my mother's face when I said guest room. "That is the way we raised you. We're proud of you, Sadie. And Jeremy?"

"Yes, ma'am?"

"Thank you for all that you do to keep our daughter and the area she lives in safe."

Jeremy might have melted a bit under my mother's charm. It wasn't hard to do. She was very gifted at appreciation and warmth. It had served her well in her career as a nurse. "Just doing my job, ma'am, but thank you for your kind words. I promise that I do everything I can to keep your daughter safe and–" he winked, "–out of trouble."

This made both my parents laugh. "Good luck with that one, young man," my father interjected.

Deciding this had gone on long enough, I said, "All right, I think it's time to say goodbye, you two. We don't want Jeremy's food to get cold, do we?"

Their mirth at my discomfort was evident, but at least they hadn't asked any more about Sydney. Hopefully, I could give them a call tomorrow evening with a really positive update. "Okay, we'll let you two enjoy your evening. Sadie, call soon, please? I want an update on your sister."

I swear that woman could read my mind. "Of course. I love you both."

"We love you, too."

Jeremy chuckled as he took a seat at the table. "They seem really nice."

"You enjoyed that a little too much. Eat your dinner."

"Yes ma'am," he winked as he started putting food on his plate.

"They're not only nice, but they're also very good people. I'm fortunate to have such amazing parents."

"You are."

We ate in companionable silence. I'd wanted to ask about his parents, but I felt like his statement closed the door for conversation on the topic. Besides, he needed some rest. Once he'd finished more than half of his dinner, he restarted the chat. "So, either JB was misinformed or your sister misunderstood."

He had my attention. "About what?"

"The remains of the batteries found weren't solid-state batteries."

"What were they?"

"Lithium-ion batteries."

"Are they more susceptible to catching fire?"

He finished the last few bites. "I'm no expert on batteries, but from what I overheard some of the others say, lithium ones require safeguards for when they need to be heated up and cooled down, more so than solid-state batteries. If those safeguards aren't there or fail, the chance of them overheating and catching on fire are very high."

"So, someone buried potentially faulty batteries in the forest and that caused the fire?"

"It appears so, though we can't really confirm if they were faulty as any evidence that they might be able to use in those findings were destroyed in the fire."

"Wow."

"Pretty much. Listen, as much as I'd love to talk about this more and work through theories..." As if to support what he was going to say next, he yawned before offering a sheepish grin.

"You need rest. Go get some sleep. When does your next shift start?"

"I have to be there at six tomorrow morning."

"Not fun. Well, you know where everything is now. I'll clean up and then get coffee ready so all you have to do is hit start. I should be awake, but given my lengthy nap this afternoon, it's going to be awhile before I go to sleep, which might require a little sleeping in. There's some leftover sausage, biscuits, and gravy in the fridge if you want that for breakfast."

"You are definitely the hostess with the mostest." Jeremy smiled as he stood and took his dishes to the sink. As he began to rinse them, he added, "Seriously, thank you for this, Sadie. You've been amazing through this entire ordeal."

I joined him at the sink with my dishes. "It's been nice having company."

This time, I was rewarded with a soft kiss on the lips, the kind a girl could get used to. "It's been nice being here," he whispered.

With that, he headed into the guest room. I finished the dishes and made myself a decaf latte before settling again in my recliner. I pondered what Sydney had told me about JB's claims and decided to make use of my phone call to her.

"Wilson Sheriff's office, how can I help you?"

Recognizing the voice, I decided to try honey instead of vinegar to catch the fly this time. "Good evening, Deputy Matthews. I trust you were able to get some rest today. I know you've been working very hard."

It took a few seconds before he responded. I don't think he was used to me being so cordial to him, and he wasn't quite sure how to respond. "A little, yeah. Guess you're calling to speak with your sister."

"If I may." Either he was tired or in shock. Either way, I'd keep playing nice as long as possible.

"Yeah, hold on."

"Thank you."

A moment later, Sydney was on the line. "Hey Sadie, thanks for calling me back."

"Sorry, it wasn't sooner. I was out trying to learn new things. Then, exhaustion won over."

"Did you have your call with Mom and Dad?"

"Yes, and thankfully Jeremy's presence at my house kept them distracted from asking too much about you. She made me promise to call with an update soon. Hopefully, by tomorrow evening, you can speak with her."

There was a long pause. "I don't think that's going to happen, but I appreciate your optimism."

I was being optimistic, so there was no reason to belabor that point. If our situations were reversed, I'd probably be in the same mental space Sydney was in right now. "You think of anything else that might help? I learned today they don't have the murder weapon, so be sure to let JT know that in the morning."

"No murder weapon? Why am I here, then? Though, I brought no weapons with me, so unless they're saying I killed him with my bare hands, I'm not sure why or how they think it was me."

"JB was shot and the killer either got away with the weapon or it's at the bottom of Lake Amore. Divers are expected tomorrow. I have a couple of my contacts trying to learn how they jumped to the conclusion of you and/or me so quickly."

"There's nothing that makes sense. I didn't kill him, Sadie."

"I know you didn't, sis. As hard as this is, please try to be patient. I promise you I'm doing what I can out here to clear your name."

She sighed. "I know, and I believe you."

It was important to give her something to focus on. "Hey, were you made privy to any internal documents from CellCo about past events that could cause a PR issue?"

"They gave me a big box of paperwork, but with being consumed with the whole situation with JB, I haven't had time to properly research it yet."

This could potentially answer some questions. "Where is the box?"

"I put the contents in the safe in the attic of the house I'm renting. Do you think something in there might help us?"

"It can't hurt, right?"

She laughed. "No, at this point unless you found the murder weapon in that box, I don't think there's anything there that could hurt."

Her statement gave me pause. If someone was trying to frame her or me, planting the murder weapon would seal the deal. The question was, if someone really was doing that, was I their target or was it Sydney? Only one way to find out. "Tell me the address."

She relayed the information, including the security code for the door and the safe. "Okay, got it. Thanks. I'll check it out. Are they treating you all right?"

"Yes, Deputy Matthews seems to have taken a liking toward me. He brought me a grilled chicken salad from The Club tonight for dinner."

My ears had to be deceiving me. "He what?"

She chuckled. "I think he's doing it so when I share, you'll be annoyed."

"He's right!" I couldn't believe that man. "Just be careful. He may try to get you to reveal information I've been unwilling to give him."

"You mean about your past?"

That's exactly what I meant. "Most likely."

She laughed. "I'd have to know something about your past, other than your childhood, to share. As I know very little, there's not much information he can get from me."

A valid point had been made. "Okay, I hear what you're saying. Just watch that one, he's slippery."

"I deal with slippery types all the time. I know how to handle them."

My sister was full of wisdom this evening. "Fair enough. Just know he's been trying to put me away for crimes I didn't commit almost since I arrived."

"He does seem to have a burr in his boots for you."

"Look at you with the Texas euphemisms. How long have you been in town again?" I teased.

"You pick up a thing or two when you have nothing to do but sit around. Now, go find some answers for both of us."

"Love you, Sydney."

"Love you, too. See you in the morning."

Looking at my phone after disconnecting the call, it revealed it was about eight in the evening. I peeked in to find Jeremy sound asleep. I closed the door and wrote a note, just in case he woke up. Didn't want him to worry. The missed call symbol still taunted me from the top of the screen. Who was the unknown caller? If it was so important, why didn't they leave a message? Due to other pressing issues, that would have to be a problem for another day. If it was that important, they'd call back.

About twenty minutes later, I arrived at Sydney's rental house. Located a few miles outside of Wilson, it was a nice, one-story home with brick and, of course, the Texas star displayed proudly on the front door and over the garage. The roof was typical of many houses in my area with steep angles. Since basements were rare in the area due to the danger of flooding, my theory was the additional space created with the angles provided much needed storage areas.

My heart skipped a beat when I noticed the marks on the door, clearly indicating someone had tried to gain entrance to the residence without a key or the code for the keypad. It was impossible to tell if they'd been successful just by looking at the marks.

Not wanting to run into someone inside, I decided to do a quick walk around the perimeter to peek through windows and check for any other signs of forced entry. Sure enough, there was a broken window next to the back door. Not much of a leap that the intruder had decided to simply break the window, reach inside, and unlock the back door. One would think if someone were going to have a rental home, they would have an alarm system or, at least, video cameras to protect their property. Maybe I'd make a recommendation to them after this was all over. My visual inspection as I made my way around the house provided a reasonable assurance that whomever had been there had come and gone.

Pulling on some latex gloves I'd brought from my kitchen, I entered the code on the front door and quickly slipped inside. No sense leaving unnecessary fingerprints. The view I'd seen from the windows didn't compare to the destruction on the inside. Drawers were opened, mattresses flipped, and furniture cushions tossed aside. Someone had been looking for something. Maybe the box of documentation Sydney mentioned? The question was...did they find it?

Though I knew where the safe was, I needed to make sure nothing—like a murder weapon—had been left behind for the police to find when the break-in was reported. I slowly walked through each room, trying to restore some sense of order to the place as I ensured no gun was hiding out there. Once I reached the kitchen, I had to admit if they'd hidden a gun, it was cleverly concealed as I couldn't find it. Maybe the documents were the only objective. Or this could have been a random break-in, no matter how unlikely that felt.

It was time to see if they'd been successful in their quest. I located the string hanging down next to the door in the kitchen that led to the garage. It connected to a trap door in the ceiling that served as an access panel to the space between the ceiling and the roof. Due to the unrelenting heat over the past month or so, it was going to be a mini inferno up there, but I had to check to see if the paperwork was there.

Pulling on the string, the wooden stairs unfolded. A quick visual check along with testing a few of the wooden slats gave me enough courage to attempt the climb. At the top, I found another string for a bare light bulb. A quick pull illuminated the area. It was reasonably clean for an attic. A few cobwebs, but no creepy-crawlies within my view. Over to the left, there was an odd-looking chest. I maneuvered myself onto the landing area and reached across to open the front panel. Inside, I could see the safe with another keypad. Thankfully, Sydney had provided me with the code. I'd been surprised it wasn't the same as the one to open the front door. It only took a moment of study to realize the design was similar to the safes one would find in a Hampton Inn or other hotel chain where each guest could choose their own code. I smiled as I entered the code: 1412. It brought about fun childhood memories.

We used to argue all the time over whose lucky number was the luckiest. Now, it seemed silly, but back then, we had a blast debating the merits of each number. Mine was twelve and hers was fourteen. Even though I was older, since this was Sydney's combination, she had made her number the first in the series. As soon as I hit the pound key, I heard the magic sound of the lock releasing. Thank goodness! Too much longer in this heat and I'd be nothing but some really great jewelry in a puddle. Given the amount of perspiration beading on my upper body and travelling south, a cool shower would be in order when I got home.

The safe contained an expandable brown file with a reasonable amount of contents. I closed it and maneuvered down the stairs to the air-conditioned kitchen. Grabbing a bottle of water from the fridge, I did a quick perusal of the contents. I didn't want to hang out in a house that was also a crime scene. There was also a chance someone might return for another look. The file appeared to be copies or microfiche printouts of newspaper clippings of CellCo from the past year or so, both good and bad press. Digging further down, I found a copy of the memo where they talked about applying for the grant from the government. Opening a text file on my phone, I typed in the date and made a note. It would help with a timeline later.

I switched over to the search engine and entered *CellCo* and *government grant*. There were several articles, but I skipped all the main papers and sources and selected one by an independent newspaper. They claimed CellCo shouldn't receive a grant for development of the new batteries since they'd yet to successfully master the lithium-ion batteries. Given the improper disposal of those batteries causing a forest fire, I had to agree with them. The article went on to say an internal source had cited lack of proper disposal and numerous safety violations. Geez, CellCo wasn't too far ahead of Lester about a year ago with the number of violations he'd racked up just since I'd been here.

I did a quick shuffle through the remaining papers to see if there were any gold flecks hiding out in the gravel. My gaze caught another internal memo. This one was from someone in operations to Scott McIntyre sharing that, thanks to an external information source, they believe they'd finally got the formula for the solid-state batteries locked in. I made a note to check to see if that timing corresponded to Future Energy Source's claim alleging their schematics had been stolen. That would make for an interesting coincidence, except I didn't believe much in them. I also noted that Scott McIntyre's name was in several of the documents, and he was copied on most of the internal memos. This man must not only serve on the board but also be heavily involved in the operations of

CellCo or a large shareholder, maybe? Either way, he was on my radar now.

It was getting late, and I needed to get home. Further sorting through these documents and making notes on my laptop would be helpful. I quickly shuffled all the papers together. I could finish looking at them later. I hit the bottom of the stack a couple of times on the table to line everything up, and an air tag along with a small, folded paper fell away from the larger stack.

I wasn't sure if Sydney put the tracking device in the folder or someone else. Until I could verify with Sydney, I twisted the back cover to remove the battery. That would keep it from transmitting. I slid it back into the file. I then opened the small paper. It was a teaser article by Elena and Edgar Romano, Emerson's parents! I quickly scanned the print. They claimed CellCo had tried to be a jack of all trades but had mastered none, and that more details would follow. I did a quick visual search, but I didn't see anything more from them. This certainly warranted further research. It made me wonder who had compiled the information for Sydney. Had this been their way of alerting someone on the outside that there was a connection between CellCo and the Romano's untimely death? I'd need to learn more, from Sydney and in general, before sharing any of this with Emerson. I didn't want to get his hopes up.

After securing the premises the best I could, I made my way slowly back to my house. Once I confirmed everything with Sydney, I could take the next steps on that branch of the investigation.

A golf cart was parked right next to my driveway when I arrived home. I placed the folder of information in the glove box and locked it before getting out. With no idea who was waiting for me in the darkness, I wasn't taking any chances. I grabbed the pepper spray from my purse and had it at the ready. Parking the truck in the drive, as I didn't want to provide easy access to my house, I cautiously approached the golf cart. The light from my phone illuminated my late-night visitor. "Jackie? What are you doing here?"

Jackie turned to me, her watery gaze prompting me to slip the pepper spray into my back pocket. "Lester's in trouble. I need your help."

Chapter Eight

I guided Jackie into the garage. It was too late to stand outside and have this conversation, but the presence of Jeremy's truck parked on the other side of the street told me he was still inside and, hopefully, asleep. Which meant going into the house wasn't really an option, either. Grabbing a bottle of water for both of us from the garage fridge, it was time to learn what was going on. "What kind of trouble?"

She shook her head. "I'm not sure, I just know it in my gut."

Instincts were valuable tools, but they were also susceptible to emotional influence. "Okay, tell me what you do know."

After a few sips of water, she exhaled slowly. "He left the marina around nine this evening."

A quick check of my watch showed it to be a little after ten. "That's barely over an hour, hardly cause for alarm." My patience had obviously taken a hit with everything going on this weekend. Had all this just started on Friday? Ugh!

Tears formed in her eyes, and I instantly regretted my impatience. Reaching out, I put my hand gently on her shoulder. "Hey, I'm sorry. It's been a long day. Tell me the rest." This was a pretty strong reaction for someone, especially an adult, to be gone only an hour.

The moisture fell freely down her cheeks. She reached into her back pocket, pulled out a piece of paper, and handed it to me. "This is why I'm so worried."

Opening the note, I read it out loud. "Sis, I've gotten myself in over my head this time. If I'm not home by midnight, I'm most likely dead. Tell Sadie and her sister I'm sorry."

My gaze found hers. "It's not midnight yet, there's still time."

Jackie's curls swayed as she shook her head. She dried her tears, took a deep breath, and stood tall. "I'm not standing around waiting for my brother to be dead. He's a pain in the butt, but he's *my* pain in the butt and I don't want anything bad to happen to him."

Nodding, I agreed. "Very understandable. Maybe we should call the police?"

"No!"

Her fierce reaction led me to believe there was more to the story—there usually was.

"The police have the means necessary to find him in the less than two hours we have left, Jackie. Why wouldn't you want their help?"

"I'm pretty sure he is involved in something illegal," she sighed. "I can't risk it just yet. I know he's no one's favorite, but he's family—the only one I really have left. I want to keep law enforcement out of it as long as possible. You said you helped people who were in bad situations. This is a bad situation, Sadie." Her gray gaze locked onto mine. "I'm asking for your help."

Me and my big mouth. However, she was right. "Okay, fair enough. First, any idea where he was going and why he wanted you to tell me and my sister he was sorry?"

"No, on both counts." She sat down heavily on a bench near the wall.

"Okay, let's go back to your theory about him doing something illegal. To us on the outside, it looked like he was straightening up his act. He brought the marina back to code, cleaning and fixing things that had been in disrepair for quite some time, and no longer having to pay fines with money no one knew he had (or where it had come from). That says to me he was getting his life right and leaning away from potentially illegal activities."

"Which," she huffed, "I'm sure is exactly what he wanted people to believe. You want to hear my theory?"

"I do." I presently had none other than what I'd just shared.

"I think he's been involved in shady dealings for some time now. Whoever was behind it used Lester and his management of the marina to keep attention away from whatever bad things they were doing in the lake or the area surrounding it. In exchange, they made sure his fines were paid and he had a little extra for his trouble."

"Seems like a reasonable theory. It's been done before and

would, no doubt, be done again. So, why the change? Did he want a clean break and now they're coming for revenge?"

"Ha!" she scoffed. "Highly unlikely. The only reason my brother would change his tactics would be if there was a bigger payday and incentive."

Based on what I'd observed of Lester, her logic was sound. "Okay, so maybe he was offered more money by someone else, so he switched tactics and now the previous people he was dealing with want retribution?"

"It's possible," she sighed, "but I think it's more likely he was running both schemes at the same time."

That was risky business. Bad guys weren't known for their willingness to get along with each other or share flunkies. "If that's the case, this is going from bad to worse. Any idea who bad guy number one and two might be?"

"Not really, but I do have this." She pulled out her phone and showed me a beautiful picture of Lake Amore as the sun was setting.

"Beautiful sunset. Not sure what I'm looking at other than that, though."

She used her fingers to zoom in. Lester was standing at the front of his houseboat with someone else. "I love sunsets, so I take pictures from all different angles at the marina, looking for the perfect shot at the perfect time. This one was taken about six months ago."

"Right when Lester started cleaning up the marina," I interjected, sensing where she might be going with this line of thought. "Who's the man he's with?"

"I'm not sure. The more I've been thinking about all of this, the more I believe this was the meeting that changed everything. The man came and left by boat, so he never walked by my shop. This is the best picture I have of him."

"You've never seen him here again?"

"No. I asked Lester about it, but he told me not to trouble my pretty little head. He wanted me to focus on my political career and not worry about anything else." She exhaled long and slow. "And so I did."

I sat down next to her on the bench. "We need to learn who that guy is, or who he represents. If they struck a business deal that night, but you haven't seen him since, he is probably high up in whatever criminal enterprise Lester went to work for. Of course, he could also be a front man the guy in charge trusts to conduct business on his behalf. Why don't you send me the picture and I'll see what I can find out?" The angle of the setting sun could cause some issues, but if anyone could find out who this person was, it was Jess.

"You just want me to text it?"

"Email is easier and keeps the quality of the photo intact." I had no idea if that was true or not, but I said it with confidence. Besides, I wanted to get this photo to Jess right away and didn't have access to my burner phone at the moment since it was in the house. I wasn't giving Jackie my personal cell number.

"Sounds good." She handed me her phone. "Just email it to yourself. My hands are shaking too much to type."

Once completed, I used my phone to forward the email to Jessica with a message: *I know I'm calling in all my favors. Can you identify the man on the right?*

A moment later, my phone dinged with a response: *Will see what I can find. No need to use a favor, but restocking my snacks is vital. Your research is a late-night activity.*

I made a mental note to place an order for the very specific snacks she required when burning the midnight oil: peach oolong soda and Kobe beef potato chips. We'd once ordered an exotic snack sampler pack from a website, and those two items had snagged Jessica hook, line, and sinker (as my father taught me when he took me fishing as a child). I kept her stocked with those items. I sent a quick reply. *Order will be placed and sent to the last PO box I have.*

I returned my attention to Jackie. "Okay, I have a friend working on the identification. Now, we need to find Lester. Any idea where he might go or where this meeting was to take place?"

Jackie stood and started to pace, the tears returning to her face. "I just don't know, Sadie. How are we going to help him if we can't find him?"

Exhaling a long breath, I sought to find the perfect balance between compassion and tough love. I stopped her pacing by putting my hands on her shoulders and waited for her to meet my gaze. "I understand how difficult this is. I need you to focus and think right now. There'll be time for emotions later. Do you have any way to know his whereabouts or contact him that won't draw attention if someone else sees it?"

Moments later, she offered a few final sniffles and her eyes cleared. "There might be something."

"We can work with something." I smiled to offer encouragement.

She reached into her back pocket to retrieve her phone. Once unlocked, she scrolled through until she pulled up an app. I moved to stand behind her to secure a better view. "This one tracks the GPS location of your phone. When Lester travelled earlier this year to New Mexico, I bugged him until he agreed to use it while he was away. Once he got home, I completely forgot about it."

"May I?"

She nodded and handed me the phone. "I've seen this kind of app before. We jokingly called it a stalker app since you can track other people."

Jackie chuckled a bit. "That's close to what Lester said." At her admission, tears formed in her eyes again.

"It looks like his GPS or maybe his phone is off. Does this program allow you to see history?"

She nodded and took the phone back. A few swipes later, she returned it to me. "It looks like he was just outside the Flying V Campground when the trail stopped."

Great. I'd never heard of this place until around forty-eight hours ago, now it had come up twice. "Then, that's where we're going."

Since her purse was already secured around her body and she only had a golf cart, she walked toward my truck. I had no issue with driving, but I felt we needed to have a bit of a game plan before we stormed the gates of the campground. "We need to know what we're going to do once we get there and have a plan if things go bad." In my experience, nothing ever went straight to plan, oftentimes not even the first several versions.

"What's to know? We go, we find Lester, and we bring him home."

Moving to stand in front of her again, I worked to keep my voice steady and even. "While I appreciate the simplicity of your plan, we have no idea who he's with, what their intentions are, and, most importantly, how many people are going to be there. We're unarmed, other than the pepper spray I keep in my truck."

"A proper Texas woman is never unarmed," she scoffed as she reached into the cross-body bag and revealed a Glock 42 that sported a pink camo design. "A gift from Lester on my twenty-first birthday."

And to think my father gifted me with my first IRA account at that age. As an investment banker and finance whiz, he'd thought it the perfect thing to give someone starting out their adult and career life. "While it's nice having for protection, we still don't have the answers necessary to go in there guns ablazin'."

Jackie returned the gun to her purse. "Fine, but if it's necessary, I won't hesitate to use it."

"Understood." Once the gun was safely put away, I continued. "We'll opt for surveillance first to see what we're up against. If he's in immediate danger, or we're outmanned and outgunned, we call the police and they send in the cavalry to save the day. Deal?"

"Deal."

I looked longingly toward the house. Jeremy was fast asleep and would only have my note about going to Sydney's rental house to pick up paperwork. I prayed we would be back, safe and sound, before he woke up. Jackie's voice brought me from my thoughts.

"Sadie? Ready?"

"Yes, let's go."

The Flying V Campground was about fifteen to twenty minutes outside of Wilson on the other side of the lake. We rode in silence for most of the way until about five minutes from our destination. Out of the corner of my eye, I saw Jackie twist in her seat toward me. "I'm sorry, Sadie."

My face scrunched in confusion. "For what?"

"For how you were treated when you first arrived in town. We tend to be suspicious of outsiders for some reason, but that's not a good excuse."

"Small towns protect their own. It's part of what draws people to them. Plus," I grinned, "It's not like I made it easy."

"Yeah," she chuckled. "Getting accused of murder in your first few weeks probably didn't help."

"Probably not," I laughed.

As we pulled up to the entrance of the campground, I turned off the headlights. With the GPS map on the display in the truck, I could follow the road without seeing it (for the most part). We needed the element of surprise as much as possible. We followed the road, keeping our eyes peeled for any sign of life.

"Sadie, over there." Jackie's urgent whisper guided my attention to a campground area right next to the lake, about a hundred feet away. Thankfully, there was tree cover between us and them that could allow us to get closer without, I prayed, being seen.

I backed the truck into another campground site on the opposite side of the road. "Okay," I started in a quiet tone, "let's follow the tree line and circle around so we can get as close as possible without being seen. You have options to use different colored lights on the flashlight app of your phone?"

"I think so." She made a few swipes, "Yes. What color should I use?"

"Red will be the best for allowing us to see without being seen. Keep it low to the ground and just in front of your feet. No talking, not even a whisper. We listen, then we return to the truck to develop our plan of action. This is reconnaissance, and we need to know what we're up against."

"Okay."

I wasn't entirely convinced that Jackie wouldn't act. "Even if we see Lester is in trouble, we need to have a solid plan before we engage. Promise?"

She hesitated. "I promise to try. He's my brother, Sadie, the only family I have. I can't let them hurt him." As if to make good on her promise, her hand went to rest over her purse where the Glock was housed.

"I understand, but please keep in mind I have family counting on me as well. I need to make it back in one piece so I can be there to support her."

My words made the necessary impression. "I understand. I'll do my very best. Rest assured, my goal is to protect Lester and you from harm."

I believed her, but I also knew that if she had to choose, he would win. And I couldn't even be mad about it. I'd do the same thing if the situations were reversed. "Okay, let's go. As quiet as possible."

She followed my lead as we made our way closer to where I assumed Lester and his cronies were hanging out. Once we were as close as we could safely get, the flashlights were turned off and we crouched down to listen.

"Where are the diamonds?"

"They're safe."

I recognized Lester's voice answering the question, but I had no idea who the other guy was. I adjusted some branches, trying to see what was going on. My line of sight showed the other man was tall and heavyset. In the darkness, I couldn't make out any other features. Lester had barely finished speaking when the man nodded. Another figure appeared out of the shadows and landed a solid blow to Lester's gut. Jackie's gasp was muffled by her hand over her mouth, but I shot her a look, anyway, with the recognized sign of my finger over my mouth sending a desperate reminder she had to be quiet. Thankfully, Lester's "Oof!" at the contact covered her gasp.

"Those are the payment for a deal that's going down at midnight tonight. I don't need them to be safe, I need them in my hands."

The man turned toward Lester so I could get a better look at his face. Using the night mode on my camera, I took a picture of his face. Maybe Jess could find something on him. It was hard to tell in the lighting, but I could swear I'd seen him before.

"You don't want me to involve my father. He doesn't handle disappointment well. If you can't get those diamonds to me in time, he's going to be very disappointed. You should know, I'm not half as scary as my old man. And as terrifying as he is, the guys we're doing this deal with...well, let me be clear, they won't just kill you, they'll send a message. You follow?"

Lester raised his hands in the universal sign of surrender. "I'll take you to them. I just need my gear."

"What gear? Where are the blasted diamonds?!" Another nod from the guy in charge prompted the enforcer to deliver a punch that sent Lester to his knees. My hand on Jackie's thigh is all that kept her from bolting straight into the fray. At the edge of my gaze, I caught a glimpse of steel in the faint light. Great, she had the gun out.

Lester coughed. "They're at the bottom of the lake. With the fire out, I can dive down and retrieve them from the little cove. I would've gotten 'em sooner, but the place was swarming with patrols from all kinds of law enforcement."

I remembered seeing the light below the water Friday evening. Could that have been him hiding the diamonds? If they really were there, it was no wonder he was anxious. He wasn't lying about the patrols being heavy. No way could he have gotten out there to retrieve them until the investigation was complete.

"Why should we believe you? You couldn't even convince the police the woman who was last seen with JB was his murderer."

It was my turn to stifle a gasp. So, that was how they got to Sydney/me so quickly. Lester provided an eyewitness account as fake as the Texas summer days are long.

"There were two of them. How could I possibly know that?!" Lester was entirely on the defensive now.

I realized I needed to ensure Lester's safety as much, if not more, than Jackie. He was the fastest way to get Sydney freed. While I might not be as terrifying as the men he was dealing with right now, I was confident in my ability to persuade him.

My neck craned forward to try to get a better lay of the land to see how many men were there. Right now, I only saw the guy who might not be the ultimate boss, but the son of the man who was in charge of whatever criminal enterprise Lester had gotten himself involved in and the enforcer delivering the punches, who I'd not been able to see clearly. That didn't mean there weren't other men nearby. I didn't see a vehicle anywhere, so they'd either parked a greater distance than we did, or they'd come in by boat.

He looked to the enforcer. "Get the boat ready." He then returned his attention to Lester. "We'll go to the marina, you grab your gear, and then you best deliver those diamonds or you're a dead man."

I leaned toward Jackie and whispered, "We need to get out of here now and beat them to the marina."

She nodded, and we stood to make our way back to the truck. I ignored the aching in my legs after squatting, even for such a short time. Great, one more thing to add to my exercise routine. We'd made it about ten feet or so when Jackie tripped over something and made a scuffling noise.

"Someone's here! Find them!"

I didn't even wait to hear the rest of the directive. I grabbed Jackie's hand and started to run. With my free hand, I reached in my pocket, unlocking and remote starting the truck. We needed every extra second we could.

We reached the truck and jumped in. I hit the accelerator the moment Jackie was inside. The headlights were turned on and we were hauling our assets out of the campground as quickly as possible. We'd just reached the main road when I saw headlights behind us. "Seatbelts!"

Once secured, I gunned it again, turning out on the main road. My heart thudded in my chest as adrenaline surged through my veins. The vehicle was close enough I could see it had a reinforced grill on the front. This just kept getting better.

"Sadie, we have to get to the marina!" Jackie screamed.

"Not until we lose these guys, otherwise we're dead as soon as we get there."

To her credit, she didn't argue. I pressed the gas pedal all the way to the floor and scoured my brain for an exit strategy that didn't end up with us dead in the next five minutes.

My body jolted as the grill assaulted my tailgate with a noisy thud. The truck, along with our bodies, lurched forward. I kept the speedometer increasing but doubted our ability to outrun them. I needed to either lose them or deal with them before we got to a more populated area.

They rammed us again while sending bullets in our direction, hitting the reinforced glass and sending a spider web of cracks along the back window. "Call nine-one-one!"

"No! No police!" Jackie screamed in return.

Another bullet hit somewhere in the bed of the truck. "You want to die instead of Lester going to jail for whatever crimes he's committed? I'm not going to be able to lose them."

"You said you helped people in trouble, Sadie. Lester and I are in trouble. Help us!"

I could hear the emotion in her voice. She was barely holding it together, not because we were in a high-speed chase with bullets flying everywhere, but because her brother's life was in danger.

A plan formed in my head. It was risky, but at this point, I wasn't sure how much longer we could count on the reinforced glass or their bad aim to keep us safe. "Okay, are you any good with that gun?"

"Do cowboys wear hats?"

Chancing a quick look in her direction, I caught her smiling as she pulled the Glock out of her purse. "Okay, you need to get in whatever position you can to get a good shot at their tires so we can end this pursuit."

"Their tires? They're trying to kill us, and you want me to take out their tires?!" The incredulity in her voice had me fighting the urge to lose my cool. "We need to stop them so they can't follow us, and we need to get to the marina. If the others are going by boat, it won't take them very long. We're already at a disadvantage. Our objective is a quick stop."

"Oh, I'll give you that." She unhooked her seatbelt and twisted until she could open the slider on the back window. Getting to her knees, she braced herself and took aim. At this point, I had to pray she'd not try to shoot them, even though a self-defense argument could be made. I would testify on her behalf without any hesitation–we were unquestioningly defending ourselves in this situation. A moment later, three successive pops sent my ears ringing. If we weren't going so fast, I'd have at least tried to cover the ear closest to the blast. I looked in the rearview mirror to see fire erupt from the hood of their truck and our pursuers fall back.

Jackie closed the window, turned around, buckled her seatbelt again, and smiled. "Shooting the engine block is far easier and just as effective, if not more, than the tires."

"Fair enough. Good shot."

"Thanks. Now, let's go rescue that sad sack of a brother of mine."

Chapter Nine

We arrived outside the marina about five minutes later. I had no idea, truthfully, what to do next. All the jobs my team and I had pulled over the past decade or so were carefully planned out with pre-job recon, a plan A, contingency plans, exit strategies, and plenty of support. Heck, we even had code words to communicate on-the-fly changes to the plan.

Now, there was me, Jackie, her Glock, and absolutely none of the other stuff I'd come to rely on before putting myself in harm's way. I took a few deep breaths in an effort to center my thoughts and come up with a way to save Lester and not get Jackie or myself killed. I heard the door open and reached out to halt Jackie's progress. "What are you doing?"

"Going to save Lester." The look she gave me bordered somewhere between incredulous and irritation.

"I'm all on board for that, but we need a plan. These guys aren't playing around."

She closed the door, which allowed me to breathe a sigh of relief. "Fine, you've got three minutes to lasso me into your corral or I'm hightailing it in there...what was it you called it? Guns ablazin'?"

Seriously, she was giving me three minutes? Might as well be thirty seconds. "Okay, you have a key card to get into the houseboat section, right?"

Jackie dug into her purse and pulled out her wallet. After sorting through some credit cards, she proudly displayed a white card with the marina logo on it. "This should do it."

I remembered the television screens with the camera feeds in the office. If we could get in there, at least we'd know what we'd be walking into. It wasn't much recon, but it was something. "Can you get into the office?"

"If I had my keys, but I don't. We don't have time for me to go get them. Lester could be gone by then."

Game time decision. I pulled my lock-picking set from my back pocket. It was like American Express—never leave home without it. I held up with a smile. "You have a Glock, and I can pick a lock."

Her gaze widened in surprise.

"If you're okay with it, that is. I just want to see how many and where they are. The security feeds should help."

Jackie chuckled. "You are just full of surprises. Okay with me as long as some time over a drink at happy hour, you tell me how you learned to do it. I mean, you've got your own set, so you must be a pro."

"It's a deal. Though, the truth will be far less exciting than you're imagining." I'd have to come up with a good cover story before our drinks, but hey, when I had more than three minutes, I was pretty darn good at works of fiction.

I killed the lights and pulled as close to the entrance of the marina in the parking lot as I reasonably felt safe. Thankfully, trees lined the parking lot so we could move under relative cover until we got to the office building. I wiped my hands on my jeans to rid my palms of the fine sheen of perspiration that had gathered thanks to the non-stop rush of adrenaline coursing through my system for the last forty minutes or so. Kneeling in front of the door, I went to work. Less than thirty seconds later, I heard the lock give. The door opened.

"Wow, you really are good. I can't wait to hear this story. Heck, I'll even buy the first round."

If this night involved me getting shot at anymore, she was buying all the rounds. Once inside, I pulled the shades while Jackie worked on the camera feeds. "There he is!" She pointed to the camera on the top right.

We saw Lester, dressed in his diving suit, flanked by the enforcer and the junior boss. There were some things one just couldn't unsee. Lester in a skintight bodysuit and flippers–yep, that was one of them. That's the stuff nightmares were made of.

"We have to stop them." Jackie, gun in hand, made her way toward the door.

"What's your plan, Jackie? 'Cause I'm pretty sure they have guns, too. I'm the only one who brought pepper spray to a gunfight."

Her hand paused on the doorknob. "I don't have one, Sadie. I just need Lester to know I tried." Her eyes were taking on water again.

"Look, I get it, but think about it. He has something they need. Only he knows where it's at. They were upset he hadn't delivered the diamonds. As much as I hate to admit it, your brother is a pretty smart criminal. He's managed to evade any legal repercussions for all his sketchy activity so far. Heck, he even had the town's people believing he'd cleaned up his act. We don't have a play here. We're outgunned and they are too close to Lester for us to get him to safety."

Her arms crossed in front of her. It wasn't usually a good sign, but given she'd taken her hand off the doorknob, I took it as a win. "Then, what do you propose we do?"

There was no good plan here. Not a Plan A, nor a Plan Z. Just an attempt to do something, do it quickly, and try not to get killed in the process. "Once they leave, let's take my boat. We'll do our best to match our sound to theirs while their engine is roaring so we can get as close as possible without them noticing us. Once they kill their motor, we'll hide on the other side of the cove where they will be. When Lester surfaces with the diamonds, we can reassess and see what they're going to do. If they deliver him home, we wait it out and, once they leave, you can go to him."

"And if they try to kill him?"

"Well, let's hope you're as good of an aim from a boat as you are from a speeding truck."

There was a gleam in her gaze one couldn't miss. I was sure she was imagining shooting these SOBs for putting her brother in harm's way. "Okay, that's probably the most reasonable approach." She pointed to a map of the lake on the wall. "We can make our approach from here. That way, even if they hear us, they won't be able to see us. I'll stay upfront since pepper spray isn't very effective when they're more than an arm's length or so away."

She said the last part with a bit more disdain than I cared for, but we could argue the merits of conceal and carry another day and time. We turned our attention back to the monitors and waited for them to head out in their boat. The moment they'd exited the line of sight of the marina, Jackie was headed out the door. I turned to follow and accidentally knocked the mouse and mousepad from the desk. The mouse lost its battery covering and its power source while the mousepad did a one-eighty and turned upside down when it hit the floor. My gaze was immediately drawn to a yellow sticky note on the back. It only took one second to realize it was the username and password for either the machines themselves or, most likely, the cloud account where all the backup was stored. I was going to need that.

"Sadie, you coming?" Jackie peeked her head back through the doorway.

"Be right out, just picking this up." Committing the information to memory, I hurried out the door. Now, all I needed to learn was the name of the company that provided the cloud backup and I would be in like Flynn...or whatever the expression was here in Texas.

Of course, all of that hinged on me not getting killed in the next thirty minutes or so.

We were out on the open water in short order. Without the lights, I was literally relying on my memory of the lake and the path Jackie had outlined on the map in the office. We were going too fast for my depth finder to alert me to trees or other obstacles lurking just below the surface. Lake Amore was a manmade lake and varied in depth from one spot to the next. I shuddered to think what one might find if they explored below the surface. Maybe if we all survived tonight, Lester could tell me what he saw when he dove for the diamonds. Hopefully, this time, it wouldn't be his life flashing before his eyes.

As we neared the outcropping of trees, I slowed the engine to allow for a quieter approach, along with the monitoring of objects below the water nearer to the shore. I handed Jackie a pair of binoculars and took out a second pair for myself. I was like a boy scout...always prepared.

I watched Lester sit on the side of the boat before falling backward into the water. I had no idea how long it would take him to retrieve the diamonds. I sent up a silent prayer that they were exactly where he left them.

After several tense minutes, Jackie whispered, "Something's wrong."

"Why? What makes you say that?"

"It's not that deep in the cove. He should've been down there and back by now."

A horrible thought crossed my mind. "You don't think he's trying to escape under the water, do you?" I stopped short of adding that only an idiot would try that. These people knew where he lived, where he worked, and, lest we forget, he had flippers on his feet, whereas they had a speed boat.

"Not even Lester is that stupid," she paused before adding, "I hope."

Oh, how I hoped so, too.

I kept my magnified vision fully focused on the small boat and the area where Lester had gone down. The men were starting to pace. The junior boss pulled out his cell to make a call, while the enforcer kept his hand resting comfortably on the gun holstered at his side. I shot a side glance at Jackie. Her pink camo weapon of targeted destruction was still in her purse–that was good news. The longer we kept the bullets from flying, the better. I checked my watch, just before eleven-thirty. Had the junior boss said midnight for the deal, or just Lester's timeline for making it back alive? Either way, it had to be soon.

A moment later, Lester broke the surface, his hand holding a box which, I assumed, contained the diamonds. The man ended his call. I could almost see the relief on his face. Whoever they were doing business with must have been front page bad news. They helped Lester into the boat and checked the box he'd retrieved. I assumed the diamonds were all accounted for because a moment later, the boat sped off.

"Sadie! Why aren't they heading back to the marina?" Jackie's frantic voice cut through any relief I'd felt in those few fleeting moments.

I turned on the engine and maneuvered out enough to follow the boat. It was risky. No lights, just trying to follow their wake trail, and hoping they didn't turn around and notice us.

Their speed increased. I had no idea if it was because they realized we were following them, they were late for the exchange, or perhaps he had a need...a need for speed. Movie quotes were not going to help the situation. I needed to focus.

"You're losing them!" Jackie shared, as if I didn't realize that detail.

"I'm operating in the dark here, and that makes going faster a little dicey."

"Just get me close enough so I can take out the engine." With those instructions, she moved toward the front of the boat and took up her firing position.

Good Lord, what had I gotten myself into? My watch lit up with an incoming text. It was Jeremy. Fantastic. I'd have to look at that later as I needed to keep my eyes ahead and not be distracted. I was sure he was just checking on me.

There was a small beach up ahead that I could see thanks to the lights dotting the shoreline. This was a place where people came to play in the lake. It certainly wasn't a place for boats to dock.

A moment later, my mouth gaped open as the boat did exactly that, running right up onto the shore. The men jumped out, pulling Lester with them as a big truck created a small sandstorm with its tires as it drove onto the beach and parked next to the men.

The sound of shots firing had me ducking and searching for the source. It hadn't looked like they had their weapons drawn. It took only a moment to realize it was Jackie. I didn't know a whole lot about guns, but I was fairly confident we weren't close enough to them yet for any high degree of accuracy from her weapon.

"What are you doing?" I yelled over the sound of the motor.

When the men heard the shots, they shoved Lester into the truck and handed the diamonds to the driver before turning their attention on us. The guns they pulled from the back of the truck looked more like automatic rifles to me. And while I couldn't swear to it, I was pretty sure they had a scope. Their accuracy would be far deadlier than Jackie's attempts. There was nothing we could do now but save ourselves.

I turned the boat toward the marina and ignored Jackie's shouts. She wasn't happy, but she at least would be alive. She ran past me to the back of the boat and continued shooting until her clip was empty. I didn't slow down, didn't pass go, and didn't collect Lester or the diamonds. Once we made it to the no-wake zone at the marina, I slowed the engine. Jackie came to stand beside me.

"They're going to kill him, and we ran away like cowards."

I exhaled slowly, trying not to let my emotions get in the way of my response. I knew her words were born out of terror rather than anger. "We were outmanned and outgunned. Lester was already in the truck. We lived to fight another day."

"And if Lester doesn't live to see another day?"

This was the hard part. I was a firm believer that we made our choices and then had to deal with the consequences, good or bad. Lester had made a long series of poor choices, which landed him in the back of that truck tonight. I knew, in my heart of hearts, that Jackie knew this as well. She didn't like it, but she knew it. "He's valuable to them. They may teach him a lesson, but I don't think they'll kill him."

I pulled into my slip and secured the boat. Jackie helped and then offered, "Let's hope you're right."

We walked through the marina in silence until we were on the public side of the gate. I felt compelled to say something. "I'm not giving up. We're going to find him. I promised I'd help, and I will."

A mirthless chuckle escaped her downturned lips. "I don't think we need your kind of help anymore. Goodnight, Sadie."

I watched her walk away and tried to understand what she reasonably thought we could have done differently. I was all about protecting the underdog, even putting myself in the line of fire. But this was different. Usually, I was protecting the good guys from the bad guys. In this case, they were all bad. That wasn't how I wanted to go out. The thought crossed my mind to go after her and try to explain. Sometimes, saying the right thing at the wrong time did more harm than good. I glanced at the office and debated picking the lock again to check the feed. Maybe I could get some answers. Moving toward the door, a sticker on the window caught my attention. It was the name of the security company. Bingo. No need to break and enter, I could log in from the safety of my living room.

My phone buzzed again. Jeremy. I had no idea how I could explain any of this to him. I answered, "Hey, I'm almost home."

"I got your note, but it didn't say what time you left, or when you thought you might be back. I woke up to get a glass of water and realized you were still gone. It's almost midnight, Sadie."

True, I hadn't dated or time stamped my note. I wasn't familiar with being accountable to another person. The fact I'd left any note at all reminded me of how special Jeremy was. "Give me five minutes. I'll be home and I'll bring you up to speed."

"Okay." His agreement sounded more like disbelief. Or maybe it was concern. When it came to my life, he had every reason to believe things weren't all sunshine and roses. Even though we hadn't officially dated yet, he'd been in my life long enough to see the circus it sometimes resembled.

Once home, I came in through the garage. Jeremy was waiting with a cup of hot, steaming liquid.

"You're giving me coffee at midnight?" My mouth quirked into a slight grin even though I knew the adrenaline coursing through my veins would be more than enough to keep me awake most, if not all, of the night.

"It's decaf."

"Oh, okay. Should we sit?"

Not waiting for an answer, I moved to sit on the couch, and he opted for the recliner. I took a long sip for courage and decided there was no need to spin a tale. I'd promised the truth, and I was going to deliver. This was the way my life went, and despite my desire to start a new chapter, I couldn't change who I was at my core. That meant I would continue to help people whenever I could. And, unfortunately, it often resulted in me putting myself in danger from time to time. If Jeremy couldn't handle that, it was best to know now.

To his credit, he kept his face neutral and didn't say anything until I finished. "So, I'm not sure what to do about Lester, but I saw the name of their cloud security on the window of the office as I was leaving. If I can get access to the security feed, I might be able to prove Sydney didn't shoot JB and maybe learn something that helps us find the people who have Lester."

"Well, you've been busy while I slept." He offered a small smile.

To be honest, I wasn't sure if that was a good sign or a bad one. I was sure I'd know in just a few minutes.

"What can I do to help?" he asked.

Those six words warmed my heart more than anything else he could have said. I reached across the space between us and took his hand. "Thank you for the offer. You have no idea how much that means to me."

"Is this where you politely decline my offer?"

I knew I was tired, but he sounded upset. Squeezing his hand, I tried again. "It's not that. I just don't know what to do. Jackie is adamant against calling the police and I know that's what you'll want to do. Heck," I chuckled, "you must be rubbing off on me, as I suggested it multiple times already."

He moved over to sit beside me and put his arm around me, pulling me close. "That's progress, I'd say."

"Very funny. At any rate, if we called the police, what would we tell them? Some unnamed men took Lester to some unnamed place in a dark truck that I don't have even a partial plate for them to run."

"I see your point. Okay, so I'm asking again, what can I do to help?"

I turned my face toward him. "You can kiss me so I can start to think straighter," I grinned.

His smile warmed my heart. "Well, I do like to protect and serve. It sounds like this qualifies for both."

My laughter was silenced the moment his mouth touched mine. The warmth made me forget all the danger of the past hour. The respite ended all too soon, but it left me feeling refreshed and refocused.

"Thank you for telling me the unaltered truth. That meant a lot."

"Well, if that's my reward for full disclosure..." I winked and offered a trademark Sadie-sassy smile.

He laughed and pushed me away. "Okay, let's figure this out."

"Fine. I'm going to make some real coffee and try to access the security footage."

Jeremy nodded. "And I'm going to get on to the county system to see if there have been any updates."

We both stood and headed toward the kitchen. "Can you..." I stopped, realizing what I was about to ask was nothing more than a hunch. Jeremy wasn't a big fan of gut instinct.

"Can I what?"

"Nothing."

"Do I have to kiss you again to get you to tell me?" He cracked a small smile.

Very tempting, but I didn't want him to think I was that kind of girl. The kind that would only tell him the truth if there was something in it for me. No matter how amazing that something was. "Well, I would never say no to a kiss from you, but this is just a hunch. I know how you feel about those."

His arms surrounded me from behind. "Hey, we're both in new territory here. If I were going to trust anyone's hunches, it would be yours."

I might be falling in love. But first, we needed to get Sydney freed, rescue Lester, and, while we were at it, if we could get to the bottom of the death of Emerson's parents, that would be pretty amazing, too. "That means a lot. Thank you." I wrapped my arms around his and basked in the comfort of his embrace for a moment longer. Finally, I turned. "I can't shake the feeling that all of this is somehow connected."

"All of what?"

"It's going to sound crazy," I warned.

"If it was completely logical, it wouldn't be a hunch."

The man had a point. "The things the men said, the way they behaved…"

"Go on, what do you think?"

"I think they're in the drug business." There, I'd said it.

"As in a cartel?"

I shrugged. "I'm not sure. If so, I would guess them to be middle management, maybe higher–at least the one giving the orders. Pretty sure his father is the boss." I tried to remember the exact words I'd heard, but the number of bullets whizzing by me earlier had affected my short-term memory. "And there's a deal going down tonight. That's why they needed Lester to get the diamonds. It was payment. I'd bet my inventory it was for drugs."

"I have a friend that works for the Houston DEA office. He might know something. Let me make some calls."

"Jeremy, you realize it's midnight, right?" I smiled. Both of our days and nights were all messed up since the fire broke out.

"Good thing DEA agents work crazy hours."

I laughed. "A good thing, indeed."

Jeremy went to make his calls while I fired up the laptop. I sent up a quick prayer that, minimally, there would be something on the security feed that would prove Sydney wasn't the killer. I logged in, thankful the info on the sticky note was, in fact, for their cloud account. It took a few minutes to learn how the footage was stored. Finally, I located the camera that pointed toward the houseboat area and, by extension, Ally's Hangout. My fingers trembled as I pulled up the fateful day in question. I referred to my notes for the approximate time of death and fast forwarded to thirty minutes before the window of opportunity. Any other day, watching the boats bob up and down in rhythm to the soft waves would have been comforting. Tonight, it fueled my impatience. I alternated my focus on the spot where Lester would have been standing to see the shooting and the scene of the crime. Though I already knew he had lied, having video proof would be necessary since our fake eyewitness wasn't available to provide an updated statement.

Fast forwarding until something happened took me about thirty minutes into the feed. I saw a person enter Ally's Hangout and sit at a picnic table. Zooming in, the picture was grainy but there was ninety-five percent certainty the man was JB. I paused the video and took a picture with my cellphone. Maybe Jess could clean it up. Hitting play, I watched him continually check over his shoulder. He was probably waiting for Sydney to arrive. A few minutes later, a woman walked up to his table. He stood and shook her hand. I zoomed in, paused, and took another picture. Though she resembled my sister in stature and hair color, this woman was curvier and a little more filled out than Syd and I in the areas that mattered most.

 My brain hurt trying to figure out why he would be meeting two different women on the same night. It didn't appear to be a romantic liaison, which I'm sure his wife would be relieved to know. They talked for a moment and then he handed her something. It was very small, and I had no way of identifying it or the contents. The woman nodded and left.

JB continued to wait. Ten minutes later, which had to have felt like a lifetime to JB since it seemed that way for me as I watched this unfold, he stood before stumbling over himself, trying to get up from the picnic table. His hands went up in a defensive gesture, or maybe it was surrender. I paused and took another picture, noting the date and time stamp as well. When I hit play again, JB went down. Though details were hard to determine, I already knew it had been a double tap to the chest.

Hitting pause again, I snapped one more picture, which proved Lester did not witness the shot. At least, not from the marina. Depending on what his statement said, this could prove he was lying. If he hadn't said he was home, then all of this was for naught. Wanting to see if there was any angle of the boat the killer had been in, I checked the other feeds. None of the saved feeds had an angle that worked. About to give up, a thought occurred to me. If I'd gone to all the trouble to falsely accuse someone else, I'd certainly delete any footage that could identify the real killer. I pulled up the recycle bin. It was a long shot, but it was worth a shot. Even a last second hail Mary scored every once in a while–that's why people kept trying them.

Pulling my bottom lip between my teeth, I clicked to see what treasures might be hidden there. Dust bunnies. Ugh. How disappointing. Not wanting to give up completely, I called Jess. She would know it wasn't a secure line, so code talk would be used.

"You keep this up and I'm going to be set with snacks for the rest of the year."

Though it was meant to sound like a joke, she and I both knew that was code for *"What do you need?"* I chuckled to play along, just in case. "At least a month or two worth. I'm sending you a link with information. Can you check and see if the trash was recently taken out?" Meaning I wanted her to check if there was any chance recently deleted items from the recycle bin were still accessible.

I opened my encrypted text messaging account and sent her the pictures I took along with the access credentials. "Sent you some cleaning tasks, too."

A moment later, she replied, "Received. Stand by."

Normally, I'd just have her text, call, or email her findings, but time was of the essence. A few minutes later, she came back on the line. "I think I found something interesting in the trash. Will let you know once I can confirm. Until then, check your email."

"Thanks, Jess. You're the best."

She laughed. "You know it!"

We disconnected the call. I'd keep the details about Lester's lying ways close at heart until the attorney could see his statement. Which reminded me...

I dialed the office number for my, and now Sydney's, attorney and left a message letting him know Lester was the alleged eyewitness that resulted in my sister's arrest. And depending on the details of the statement, I might have photographic proof he was lying.

"Find what you needed?" Jeremy walked back into the room just as I hung up.

"Maybe. You?"

"I left a message for my contact. Hopefully, we'll hear back soon."

"I just got an email from a colleague who is also working on some other details for me." Not wanting to delay any longer, I pulled up the email. There were two attachments. Those had to be the cleaned-up pictures. The email contained one sentence: *Will send anything relevant once I can recover the deleted files.*

I opened the first one. It was definitely JB Nester. The second one was the picture of JB and the mystery woman. Jess had included a note: *Carmen DeSantis, head of R&D for FES.*

"Why was JB meeting with Ms. DeSantis?" Jeremy asked as he peered over my shoulder.

"You know her?" I didn't mean for my voice to be tinged with a tad bit of jealousy, but there it was.

He laughed. "Not really. She's been on the news and in the papers lately."

"Why?" I was obviously behind in keeping up with the current news. Maybe I'd come to rely too much on Kelsey to keep me up to speed on all things going on in our little part of the world.

"FES was one of the first in the state to develop solid-state batteries. They worked closely with the local government to ensure compliance with all EPA regulations, et cetera."

My gaze narrowed. "So, you know her purely in a professional capacity."

His arms surrounded me, momentarily making me forget about all the drama. "Sadie Sabatini, you're the only woman I'm interested in knowing on a deeper, personal level.'"

Turning my head so I could reach his lips, I kissed him. Not quick, not long, just right. "Let's keep it that way," I smiled.

"Promise. Now that that's out of the way, we now know that the night JB was killed, he met with Carmen."

"And according to what Sydney told me, she was supposed to be meeting him that night, too."

"For proof about the disposal of the batteries."

"Yes."

Before I could speculate further, my phone dinged. It was an encrypted text from Jess. I opened it, praying again for good news.

Man in both photos you sent previously is Don Seymore, Jr. Son of the boss of the Big D cartel. Responsible for recent influx of candy in your store. Bad news on steroids.

Chapter Ten

"What was the text?" Jeremy asked as he refilled my coffee cup before sitting down next to me.

"My colleague confirmed that one of the men at the site of Lester's abduction was Don Seymore, Jr. of the Big D drug cartel."

"Let me text my guy to see what else he can tell us."

"Sounds good." I also replied to Jess, thanking her and asking if she could uncover any additional intel. It never hurt to have more than one person looking, right?

Jeremy put his phone down with a yawn. "Okay, so Lester gives false testimony against your sister and is working for a drug cartel. So, how does JB figure into that? Did he know something about their drug trade? I know I'm tired, but I'm not seeing the connection."

I sighed. "I'm not sure. There's nothing to tie JB to any drug-related incidents, but if Lester falsely ID'd my sister, if he didn't do that for the cartel, then who?" My head started to throb again.

"Unknown. I just know we're not going to have any additional revelations without additional intel and some sleep. Do you think you'll be able to get some rest?"

I'd probably rest better if I was snuggled up to Jeremy, but I was pretty sure that wasn't in the cards. "I'm sure exhaustion will take over at some point."

He nodded, stood, and stretched before pulling me into a hug. "Please try and get some rest. We both need to be fresh for the challenges of tomorrow."

"Don't you mean later today?" I teased from the comfort of his embrace.

"Ugh, don't remind me." He kissed me quickly. "Goodnight or good morning, Sadie."

Sadly, we went to our separate rooms and settled in for the night.

* * *

When I woke in the morning, Jeremy had already left. I'd finally given in and taken some melatonin after tossing and turning for an hour or so. It must have kicked in and rendered me unable to hear him leaving for work, but he'd left a note next to the coffee pot. *Thanks for everything, Sadie. I promise to make it up to you. I'll keep you posted if I learn anything. You do the same. Jeremy.*

Not highly romantic, but it worked. No time for any romance today, anyway. I needed to get my sister freed and untangle the rest of this web of chaos. Then, and only then, could I focus on my relationship with Jeremy. I really wanted to have that official first date.

An hour later, I walked into Wilson's sheriff's office. I was a little early, but I was hoping to get a moment with JT before he went in to see Sydney. Instead, I found none other than Robert Birmingham seated in one of the hard-backed chairs. He was the last person I expected to see. "Hello, Robert. What brings you to this fine establishment on a Monday morning?"

Robert looked up from his paper at the sound of my voice, and his face held a look of surprise. "I think the more important question, ma'am, is how are you out here talking to me?"

Obviously, Robert hadn't received the news that I had a twin sister. I chuckled. "I'm guessing you're not feeling quite as sure about your testimony of allegedly seeing me with JB at the Flying V on Friday night, are you?"

The look on his face was priceless. Truly, I wished I had my phone out where I could snap a picture. "I...well...I...I know it was you!"

"Well, as you say, since I'm out here rather than back there with an attorney, it might make you second guess that knowledge. Though, in all fairness, he is my attorney, too. Still, I hope you'll rethink whatever you came here to tell the chief. You're not the kind of man to give false witness. I confess I'm curious why you would be seen out in public with Estelle. Honestly, Robert, why would you risk it? I can't imagine you doing it to try and catch me. I can't rank that high on your problem list. What will Dora Lee think?"

Robert's spine straightened as he stood from the chair. "You would do well to mind your own business."

I stood a little taller, too. No sense letting him have all the non-verbal fun. "I have no problem doing that, sir, until others try to involve me in whatever games they are playing with other people's lives. And I certainly won't mind my own business when someone has seen fit to weave me into their tale of fiction." I figured that was better than outright calling him a liar. I really did prefer to stay on the Birminghams' good side. They did make it challenging for me, though.

"We had nothing to do with that business with Emma Jane!"

It was an interesting choice of pronoun he used. Again, Robert didn't do anything without purpose. When he said *we*, I was sure he meant it. The bigger question was, who made up that "we?" Was it him and Dora Lee or others? Since he brought up Emma Jane, I was reminded of her maiden name: McIntyre. What were the odds that my former nemesis, Emma Jane McIntyre Birmingham, was related to Scott McIntyre? I figured it couldn't hurt to ask since Robert was already upset. "Is Emma Jane related to Scott McIntyre."

Robert paled at the mention of Scott's name. I think he realized his outburst helped me make the connection. Whatever emotion he was experiencing from his prior statement was covered up with righteous indignation. "I will repeat myself only once more, ma'am. Mind your own danged business!"

"Such language," I clicked my tongue. "No worries, that's what Google is for. A simple search will tell me all I need to know." To prove my point, I pulled out my phone and began to type in his name.

"Fine! Scott is her father."

"Interesting. Well, since your children are married...wait, they are still married, right?"

"Ms. Sabatini, I'm warning you."

Oh, how I loved being warned–not. I typically took it as a challenge. "Since you're practically family, you and Scott must be drinking buddies."

He returned to his chair with a large exhale, taking a large portion of his fight with him. "We might share a scotch and cigar from time to time, but to characterize our relationship as buddies would be a misnomer."

Since Robert had confirmed the connection, I decided a different Google search was needed. A few keystrokes later, I learned that while the Birminghams were very well off, when comparing their net worth to the McIntyres, they lost by a reasonable amount of zeroes. I sat quietly for a few moments, absorbing all this information, and decided not to point out that he must be a few rungs behind Scott on the societal ladder. That couldn't be an easy pill for him to swallow. After a minute or so, I'd decided on how I wanted to proceed. "If I tell you why I'm out here instead of back there, will you tell me why you risked so much to *see* me at the campground?" I made air quotes with my fingers.

His head shook. "You wouldn't understand."

"Perhaps not, but I understand enough about you to know you never do anything without a reason. Given all you were putting on the line, there had to be significant motivation." I'd have to find a way to thank EZ for this insight without telling her how I used it.

Robert removed his jacket and loosened his tie. I noticed dabs of moisture above his brow. The top three buttons of his white dress shirt were unbuttoned. "Is it hot in here?"

I moved over to sit next to him, noting his flushed appearance. "I think it's you. Here, drink some water. Nice slow sips." I handed him a fresh bottle of water from my purse.

"Thank you, ma'am."

"You're welcome, sir." I loved how we could hit the pause button on our little argument and play all nice with Southern manners when the situation called for it.

A moment later his phone rang. He answered it. "Hello?"

I couldn't make out what the other person was saying, but I decided I'd keep trying.

"Yes, I'm at the station." Robert paused while the person apparently asked another question. "Not yet." Another pause, and I watched Robert's demeanor change. "Something isn't right. I don't think this is a good idea."

I still couldn't make out the words, but the person on the other end was reading Robert the riot act. He exhaled slowly. "I understand. Yes, goodbye."

He put the phone down, but I was certain his blood pressure was rising. He looked agitated and his face flushed a deeper shade of red as the sweating resumed. "Robert? Are you all right? Who was on the phone?"

"Just an old friend."

My eyebrows arched. "An old friend giving you orders, it sounded like. With all due respect, I didn't think there was anyone high enough on the social chain to give you orders." I added with a smile and an attempt to calm him, "Except maybe Dora Lee."

My words had the intended effect, and he offered a small smile. "Not many besides her, it's true."

Perhaps Scott McIntyre was high enough to apply pressure to Robert?

We enjoyed the respite from the tension for a few seconds before Robert grabbed his left arm and a groan of pain emitted from his tight lips. It didn't take a medically trained person to realize something was seriously wrong. Pulling my phone out to call 911, I remembered I was technically at a police station. I banged on the door. "Hey, we need help out here!"

Deputy Matthews flung the door open. "What in tarnation is going on? What did you do?"

Ignoring his accusation, I moved to the chair next to Robert's as he started to slump over, and I didn't want him to fall. "Mr. Birmingham needs medical attention! I think he's having a heart attack."

"Well, why didn't you say so?" He pressed the button on the radio clipped to his belt. "Medical emergency at the Wilson sheriff's office. Please send an ambulance stat."

Hearing the call, Robert stood. "No need to fuss. I'm fine, really. Just a little heartburn from..." Before he could finish the sentence, he crumpled to the floor.

I immediately dropped beside him and pulled his head onto my lap. I grabbed my grandfather's handkerchief out of my purse and poured some water on it to lay on his forehead. I also grabbed an aspirin from the first aid kit in my purse. Lifting his head carefully, I encouraged him to take it. "Here, this will help."

Robert opened his mouth enough to allow me to slip the tiny pill in, then I lifted the water bottle to his lips. "Just a few sips to wash the medicine down."

He complied without a word. I could feel Deputy Matthews standing over me, watching every move I made. If Robert ended up dying, I had no doubts the deputy would testify that my administration of first aid had precipitated his death. Confident I'd done all I could do, I simply held his head in my lap. "Help is on the way, hang on," I whispered.

His eyes opened for a moment and he beckoned me close with his index finger. I leaned down. "I'm sorry," he said

My gaze widened at his apology. I assumed it was for whatever he was going to give a statement about today, but that was only a guess.

"I had no choice," he whispered.

Not wanting him in any more distress, I smiled gently. "Shhh, it's okay. Just hang in there."

"Tell EZ to lay low..."

Again, I had no idea what he meant, but I saw no reason I couldn't honor his request. "Okay, I will."

"Tell my son..."

He started to fade, so I squeezed his shoulders gently. "Tell him what, Robert?"

"The oath."

I looked up to Detective Matthews, who was still standing over us. He simply shrugged his shoulders. Why I'd thought he'd be any help was anyone's guess. I looked back to Robert. His eyes were starting to close again. "Robert, I don't understand what you mean. What oath?"

He wasn't able to answer as his head lolled to one side and he became unresponsive. "Where's the ambulance?!" I shouted. Wilson wasn't that big, what was taking them so long?

At that moment, Chief Parker ran out. "What's going on?"

"I think he had a panic attack, Chief, and then a heart attack."

"She was aggravating him!" Matthews chimed in.

If looks could kill, I'd have been on the hook for Deputy Matthews' murder as I did nothing to disguise my irritation with him. Fortunately for both of us, the paramedics arrived. I briefed them on the timeline and series of events as they lifted Robert onto the stretcher. "Understood, thank you, ma'am."

Once they were gone, the room was eerily quiet. The chief, Deputy Matthews, and I all stood processing what just happened. Remembering the last thing the deputy said, I turned to him. "Seriously, what is your problem with me?"

His shoulders moved up and down in his characteristic shrug. "Trouble just seems to follow you." He paused, probably for effect. "And I ain't a fan of trouble."

There were teeth marks in my tongue from biting back a smart retort that involved pointing out working in law enforcement probably wasn't the best place for someone who didn't like being around trouble. However, my attorney appeared from behind the door and saved me from ending up in county lockup. "Hi, JT, how'd it go?"

The attorney smiled. "Well, she's given her official statement, which is technically all they were holding her for. She's free to go for now. But she can't leave town."

"But..." I wanted to share all about the proof that would, once and for all, put this behind her.

"We'll talk in my office."

Understanding he didn't want to fully play our hand in front of the officers present, I nodded. "Should I call and make an appointment?"

JT smiled, realizing I'd caught on. "I made one for three o'clock today. I trust that gives you enough time to get your sister settled and take care of whatever you need to?"

Oh, there was plenty I needed to take care of, that was for sure. As it was only a little after nine in the morning, it should provide sufficient time. "We'll be there. Thank you, JT."

"That's what you pay me for," he laughed. "I'll see you at three."

JT shook the chief's hand. "Pleasure doing business with you as always, Chief."

The chief smiled. "Always, Mr. Thomas."

"Aww, come on, no one calls me that. My dad wouldn't even let you get away with that."

"How about your Grandpappy?" Chief Parker teased.

"He might be okay with it."

"You come from a long line of fine Southern gentlemen."

JT nodded. "Who all would remind you I need that statement emailed to me before noon."

He smiled. "Of course. It will be waiting in your inbox."

"I appreciate you. I'm going to head out. Ms. Sadie, I'll see you and your sister at three."

After JT left, I waited for Sydney to be freed. Deputy Matthews had returned to his inner office. I assumed it was to process any paperwork. Or maybe he was availing himself of one more opportunity to try to get information from Sydney. Either way, I had some information I wanted to get as well. "Chief?"

"Yes, Ms. Sabatini."

"Why was Robert Birmingham at the station this morning?"

"You know I'm not at liberty to say."

Perhaps that was true, but I couldn't help but take the liberty to say what I needed him to know. "If he was here to offer testimony about seeing me or my sister at Flying V on Friday night with JB, you should know you're going to encounter the same reasonable doubt with his eyewitness account as you did with the testimony you relied on for your arrest warrant."

"I appreciate the heads up."

JT wouldn't have been pleased that I shared that insight, but the chief was a by-the-book kind of guy. At least with this knowledge, he might question the veracity of Robert's statement if he ended up giving it. At least, I knew now, Robert had wanted to change his mind and not do whatever he'd come there to do.

I was saved from saying anything more as Sydney appeared in the waiting room. "Sydney!" I rushed up and gave her a hug.

"Hey, Sadie. Good to see you on this side of freedom."

"Let's get outta here." I grabbed her overnight bag and looped my arm through hers. "We have a lot to do today."

Sydney smiled. "Hopefully a shower and espresso is at the top of that list."

"You bet." I turned back toward the man still standing near the door. "Thanks, Chief."

"You ladies have a nice day. See you soon."

"Let's hope not," I laughed as we made our escape.

Once outside, JT was still in the parking lot. "I thought you were headed to the office."

"I am. I just had to take a phone call before hitting traffic. Try not to hand our playbook to the other team before game time, okay?"

Besides coming from a long line of attorneys, JT Thomas III also came from a long line of Aggie (or Texas A&M) football players. He loved football references. Before I could say anything, Sydney piped up, "Too late, she's already warned them about Robert's testimony."

JT shook his head. "I can't leave you alone for two minutes."

I shot Sydney a quick glare before taking a page out of Deputy Matthew's playbook and shrugging my shoulders. "I was still hyped up on adrenaline from Robert's heart attack. Plus, while I was tending to him, he whispered to me that he was sorry and that he had no choice. I have no idea what he's talking about, but I figure bearing false witness is an ideal place to start."

"It's possible, but let's not do their work for them, okay?"

Properly chastised, I sighed, "Okay."

"I'm confident we'll destroy any alleged evidence they try to establish against your sister. Speaking of which, please send me the proof you mentioned in your message along with whatever else you have so I can review it along with the statement the chief is sending. That should end this once and for all."

"I'll send what I have right away. There might be more, but I'm still waiting on my source. Thanks, JT."

"A source who is obtaining whatever this evidence may be by legitimate means, right?"

Eh, this was more of a gray area. I had the username and password, so she wasn't hacking. However, it wasn't like we had permission to be poking around. "We'll cross that bridge later, if needed."

"Sadie..." he warned.

"It's legit information, but given how I obtained it, you might have to find a way to ask for it if we get to court and the discovery phase of the evidence gathering. Nothing a competent attorney like yourself can't handle." I added a smile at the end to show the confidence I had in his abilities.

"We will cross that bridge when and if we get there. Otherwise, I don't want to know anything more about this. Understood?"

"Understood. See you at three."

We said goodbye to JT, then Sydney and I headed for the house. "I'm going to drop you off for your shower and caffeine while I run a couple errands. There's plenty of food in the fridge, both comfort and healthy, so you can choose whatever sounds good."

"You're leaving me?"

We pulled into the driveway just as she asked her question. I turned in the seat to face her. "Robert gave me some messages to deliver. I want–no need–to do that quickly while it's still fresh. I promise to tell you everything when I get home. I shouldn't be gone long. It may help your case. Even more than that, I hope it helps me see how all of this is connected."

"What do you mean?"

"For Robert Birmingham to be involved in any way, there has to be a bigger picture at play. Between the issue with the batteries at CellCo and JB's murder, along with the drug angle, Lester, and possibly the cartel, I'm trying to determine if they're connected somehow." I'd almost added Emerson's parents in there, but I needed more intel on that. Which prompted me to ask, "Who put together the information for you that was in the safe?"

"I think the executive assistant to the CEO pulled it together, but JB delivered it to me on Friday afternoon. Why?"

I reached across the cab of the truck and opened the glove box to retrieve the file of information. Pulling out the article, I handed it to her. "This was written by the parents of a young man I've come to know here in Wilson. They died tragically in an alleged boating incident not long after this article was printed. The rest of the story didn't happen."

She read over the article before handing it back to me. "And you think it's somehow linked to all this?"

"I don't know how, but yes. Why would the CEO want or even allow you to see this?" I was operating under the assumption the CEO reviewed the contents of everything that was to be delivered to Sydney and JB slipped it in there as he delivered the contents.

"I have no idea if he would or wouldn't. Why would JB think I would know or even care about the Romanos or the article they were going to write, especially if the story never saw the light of day?"

"That's the thing, though. I learned yesterday the only reason no one else picked up the story was because their research went missing. Maybe it was a hunch the Romanos had and no one else wanted to pursue it after they died? Or maybe I'm looking for threads to connect things that aren't really there. There are tons of possibilities. This is just one of them."

Sydney sat there for a moment, and I could tell she was thinking hard. "I'm not saying this is a reason but..."

"But what?" I'd take anything at this point to help me connect the dots.

"I have a bit of a reputation," she admitted.

"Oh? Care to share more?" I asked teasingly.

She chuckled. "Not *that* kind of reputation, but more of one for leaving no stone unturned. That's part of why I'm so good at my job. People know I will dig into the tiniest details and, if necessary, exploit them to my client's advantage."

"I'd love to hear some examples once this is all over. In the meantime, let's assume that the CEO knew of your reputation. I can't see any upside to him sharing something with you that would have you uncovering the details which could land them in hot water if they had anything to do with the Romanos' death." I paused for a moment. "Unless they wanted to learn if anything was there to be found and then use the NDA to keep you quiet."

She shot me a look of dismay. "I know I might have been reluctant to violate an NDA to save my own skin, but if I'd learned a client was behind the murder of two innocent people, you better believe I'd turn them in and take the consequences."

Maybe my sister and I were more alike than I thought. We both would sacrifice to help protect others. Though, I wouldn't let a piece of paper telling me I had to stay quiet keep me from saving my own skin as well. "Good to hear," I smiled. "So, if they reached that same conclusion, it makes the most sense that JB slipped it in there prior to delivering it to you."

"I suppose that's a possibility."

"What about the air tag?"

She grimaced. "I thought about it after I sent you to the house to look for everything, but I had no way of contacting you to warn you. Deputy Matthews might have been nice to me, but no way would he let me call you. What did you do with it?"

"I deactivated it until I could learn if it was you or some unnamed bad guys that put it in there. I'm glad it was you, though."

"With how JB was acting, I worried the bad guys might come to get it, so I wanted to have at least a chance at finding it if that happened."

We really were still so alike after all these years, despite being apart. "Very creative. I like it. Can you send me the info so I can track it, too? Just in case."

"Sure, I'll reactivate it and then send the information over. Now, I need proper caffeine to think clearly. You go do what you need to. I'm going to shower, get some coffee, and then I'll do some research with my sources to see if I can learn more about this."

I reached across and hugged her. "Thanks, sis, you're the best."

"Don't you ever forget it." She laughed.

Once I got her settled and the perimeter alarm set–hey, I wasn't taking any chances–I headed to the RV park situated in an unincorporated part of Wilson where EZ lived. Thankfully, her vehicle was there. I started to make my way to her front door when I saw puffs of smoke over at the dock. As smoking and watching the lake were two of her favorite things, it was a pretty safe bet it was her. I sat down in the Adirondack chair next to hers. "Hey, EZ."

"Hey, Sadie. What brings you to this side of the tracks?"

"Bad news, I'm afraid."

She turned in her chair to face me before taking a long draw on her cigarette. "What happened? Your sister get arrested?"

Shaking my head, I reached over and took her hand. "I was at the station this morning to hopefully get Sydney released. Robert was there."

At the mention of his name, her gaze widened and she put out the cigarette. "Why was he there?"

"I don't know. Though, I was hoping you might be able to tell me. But I didn't come to get information, I came to give you some. While we were talking, he got a phone call that upset him greatly. What started out as a panic attack turned into a heart attack."

The hand I was holding started to tremble. "Is he okay?"

"I'm sorry, I don't know that, either. He was unconscious by the time the ambulance arrived. I'll see what I can find out and let you know."

She pulled her hand away as she waved it in dismissal. "I appreciate that, but I have some friends at the hospital. I can ask them. Did they take him to Methodist?"

"I believe so, but I can't be certain."

She nodded and turned back to the lake as she reached for another cigarette. I gave her a minute before adding, "I'm sorry. This must be so hard on you."

Her shoulders moved imperceptibly. "I knew what I was getting into when I started a friendship with him."

"Still, it must be hard." A chance to learn more about the nature of their relationship knocked relentlessly on the edges of my brain. Figuring the worse she could do was tell me to get lost, I continued. "Has it been worth it all these years? Always being the other woman?"

I noticed a tear running down her cheek. She really loved him. Loved him and couldn't have him. I felt a pang of deep sympathy for her. "I'm not naïve. I knew from the beginning he would never leave his wife, and, truthfully, I didn't want to be a homewrecker." She turned to look at me. "Despite all the rumors, Robert, Dora Lee, and I know the truth– we're just friends. I love him deeply, but I know that we have to keep our friendship as low profile as possible. That's the deal. He and Dora Lee make a great team in society, and that works for them. Robert and I make a great team otherwise. We both fill a need in his life."

To me, it felt selfish on Robert's part, but who was I to judge? "You deserve love and a relationship that gives you all you need and want."

"I knew the moment I chose my career I was letting that pipe dream go."

"You could still make it a reality," I offered without as much conviction as I'd wanted to convey.

She laughed, a hollow sound with a bitter tint. "You and I both know that's not going to happen."

We sat in companionable silence for another minute or so when I remembered my true reason for being here. "Robert asked me to give you a message before they took him away."

"What was it?" I had her undivided attention again.

"He wanted me to tell you to lay low. Any idea what that means?"

The color drained from her face. "It means if they didn't get what they wanted from him, they would come after me next."

Chapter Eleven

"What is it they, whoever *they* are, want?" I asked a visibly shaken EZ as my hand went to cover hers.

She took a long drag of her cigarette. "I'm not sure. Robert occasionally mentions some society club he's in and wants out of, but apparently he can't. I don't understand what he's talking about, but it's a good chance they're the ones who gave him his marching orders."

"A club?"

"Yeah, I don't know. I focus more on the tone of his voice when he's rambling like that rather than the actual words."

There was so much I wanted to say but knew it would miss the mark. EZ was adept at being a very good listener and hearing things no one else even thought she was paying attention to. So, either she really had tuned Robert out, or, more likely, she knew and wasn't going to tell me. "If that's the way you want to play this, fine."

Her gaze snapped to mine. "What's that supposed to mean?"

"I come here to give you a warning, while leaving my sister at home alone, and you give me generalities and nothing that really helps."

"How could this help you?"

I stood and exhaled a long breath. "I don't know, EZ, but that's my point. Right now, someone is trying to frame me or my sister. I feel like they're using Robert and Lester to do that, and now maybe you. I'm very short on information to connect anything to anyone. Plus," I turned to her with an earnest gaze, "I can't help you if I don't know what we're up against."

She cracked a small smile. "Sure doesn't take much to get you worked up. I kind of like that about you, though."

Despite the situation, I couldn't help but grin. "Well, Italians are known for being passionate."

"Ha! Don't I know it."

I wasn't sure I wanted to know about her experience with passionate Italians, since it was probably knowledge she gained in her line of work. Before I could find something to say in return, she continued.

"Look, if it helps any, from what I could tell, Robert was sent to Flying V to keep an eye on JB, not you or your sister. I think she was a lucky convenience for someone who could then use it to frame you for his murder later."

That was an angle I kicked myself for not having considered yet. Though, with the fire, Jeremy, Emerson's situation, and everything else, I guess I could give myself a little slack for missing the possibility. "Who would want him to keep an eye on JB, and what would they want from you now?"

She took another long draw on the cigarette. I guessed it was in an effort to calm her nerves, or maybe she just liked making me wait. "I'm guessing whatever they wanted Robert to do, they'll want me to do now since I was with him the night we watched JB."

"Any idea who *they* are?" I'd already asked this question and not gotten an answer, but I figured I'd try one last time.

She shook her head. "No."

I cocked my head, shooting her a look of disbelief. "Fine."

She moved forward in her chair and turned toward me. "I'm telling you the truth, Sadie. I know it's gotta be someone with significant power if they have Robert doing their bidding. Either that or he owes them the biggest favor ever. Think about it."

It made sense. Robert wouldn't be doing just anyone's bidding. "Do you think they told him he had to bring you with him to tail JB or my sister or whatever the goal was?"

She chuckled. "No way would he have taken me out like that otherwise."

A fair point had been made. "I wonder if it was the same person who called Robert before he had his heart attack."

EZ stood and snuffed out the remains of her cigarette with more force than necessary. "Well, should they come calling wanting something from me, they will find I care far less about my reputation than Robert does. And," her intense gaze found mine once again, "I'm not very good at doing what I'm told."

I left EZ staring out at the water after I offered a brief hug of encouragement. I knew she was brave, but I also knew that whoever *they* were would most likely leverage Robert against her rather than threaten her directly. I know that's the approach I would've taken back in the early days.

With nothing more to share or gain from my interaction with EZ, my next stop was The First Bank of Texas. Thankfully, I had an ally already stationed there. In addition to being my best friend here in Wilson, Kelsey worked there as an investment banker. I also happened to be a client.

It was pretty quiet this time of day at the bank with most people being at work. I thought about my shop. Tesoro would be closed today and perhaps tomorrow depending on how all of this went down. Peeking in Kelsey's office, she was hard at work behind her computer. I knocked on her door. "Hey."

She stood and came to give me a hug. "Hey, what brings you here? How's your sister?"

I filled her in on Sydney's current status and finished with, "We have an appointment with JT this afternoon."

She looked at her watch. "Well, I don't want to take too much of your time. What brings you to the bank today?"

My smile faded. "I need to talk to Ted."

Kelsey's expression turned serious. "He's had his door shut for the last hour. I'm not sure I should disturb him."

I appreciated the delicate way she was approaching this. The last time she'd sent me into his office, I'd grilled him and his father about personal family business. It had turned out okay, but she wasn't one to tempt fate. "I understand, but I have a message for him from his father."

She looked at me with more disbelief than I wanted to see on my BFF's face. "Robert gave you a message for Ted?"

I chuckled a bit. "Well, in fairness, I was trying to save his life, so it was either me or Deputy Matthews, who was standing over me."

"What happened? Robert's life is in danger?"

In my haste to get to Ted, I hadn't given the whole story to Kelsey earlier, only specifically answered her about Sydney. I fixed my mistake and gave her the details about Robert's situation. Once I finished, she nodded. "Follow me."

She knocked softly on his door. "Mr. Birmingham, you have a visitor."

Strain was evident on his face, but he offered a small smile. "Thank you, Kelsey. Ms. Sabatini, what can I do to help you?"

"I'll see you when you're done, Sadie?" Kelsey whispered.

I nodded and stepped inside Ted's private sanctum. He stood and gestured to a chair in front of his desk. "Please have a seat."

Deciding where to start was tricky, so I decided to hedge my bets. "You've probably already heard about your father's medical scare this morning."

His gaze widened. "I have not. What happened?"

I couldn't believe his mother hadn't at least called him. I filled him in. The moment I stopped, he picked up his cellphone. I waited to see if he asked me to leave. When he gave no indication I needed to give him privacy, I remained quiet and listened to his side of the conversation.

"Mother, why didn't you call me about him?"

Since I couldn't hear what she said, I watched his body language and facial expressions carefully.

"Yes. Ms. Sabatini is here. Really? Okay, I'll tell her. Tell him I'll be over as soon as I can get away from the bank."

After he hung up, I decided to restart our conversation. "How's your father?"

He offered me a tight smile. "Mother says we have you to thank for the fact he survived. He is anticipated to make a full recovery."

I waved off his statement. "I did what any person would do."

"Oh, I'm not sure any person would understand the importance of administering aspirin to a heart attack victim, much less have one easily accessible on their person."

"What can I say? I'm like the Scouts, always prepared. I'm glad I was able to help."

He nodded. "So, besides bringing me into a loop my mother saw fit to leave me out of, is there another reason you're here?"

"I'm sure Dora Lee was busy dealing with the hospital and would have called at her first opportunity."

He offered another tight smile. "That's sweet of you to say, ma'am."

Truthfully, I thought it was terrible she hadn't called him right away. I assumed she had, otherwise I would have put a call into him to let him know. "I'm sorry I wasn't able to get to you sooner."

Ted waved my apology off. "You came, and you helped my father. That's enough."

Leaning forward in the chair, I folded my hands on his desk, wanting my body language to convey compassion and sincerity. "Just before the paramedics arrived, your father asked me to tell you something."

"What was it?"

Exhaling slowly, I shared, "He wanted you to remember the oath."

His gaze widened. It was obvious he had at least some idea what I was talking about. I still had none, and my visit with EZ hadn't produced much information as to who was behind Robert's elevated stress. Offering a sympathetic smile, I added, "I assumed you'd know what that meant, but I admit to being curious."

Ted sat quietly for another minute or so before sighing, "I can't believe he still takes that oath seriously. There's a time and place for most things under the sun. Its time has passed."

If he thought that shed light on my confusion, he was mistaken. My position remained solidly in the dark. "I can respect if you don't want to tell me." Chuckling, I added, "Sounds like something from the good ol' boys club or the mafia."

Ted laughed, "You're pretty close." He paused briefly before leaning forward. "Since you saved my father's life, sparing me from having to become an active part of that club, I can tell you a little something."

Who knew? Sometimes our good deeds were rewarded in short order. Though it wasn't the reason for my offer of help, I'd certainly appreciate the information it brought me. "I'm all ears."

"The origin of the Diamantes was pure and their goals honorable. Mostly, they wanted to preserve the Texas way of life, protect ranchers, and, of course, the oil and gas industry."

"Sounds like decent objectives, but you said started, past tense."

"Right. It didn't take long before those in positions of power used the network to further their personal agendas, trade favors, and shut down enemies."

Not surprising. Power tended to go to people's heads, and self-serving interests were always the first order of business. "So, where did the oath come in?"

The sound of bitter laughter filled the office. "To be there for each other and support their fellow members by any means necessary."

That sounded good up until the last phrase. By any means necessary left a great deal open to interpretation. "So, your father was engaged in helping one of his cronies, and now he expects you to do whatever it is or was?"

"I'm certain that's the expectation." He rose from his chair. "Thank you for coming by, Ms. Sabatini."

It was adorable he thought I'd be dismissed that easily. It was like he didn't know me at all, and I knew that wasn't the case. "Was your father at the police station this morning to offer testimony about JB?" The more I thought about it, neither Robert nor his cronies would care about me or my sister, especially since they didn't know she even existed until a day or so ago. Of course, EZ's thought that we were just a fortunate coincidence was very much a possibility. A convenient scapegoat was always good for a plan.

He shot me a look of irritation. "I don't know. My parents didn't let me in on those details. Given the phone call a few minutes ago, that should come as no surprise to you." Bitterness and resentment laced his words.

Something told me even if he knew, he wouldn't share. Being a good Samaritan only got me so far. "Fair enough. Thank you for seeing me. I'm sure I'm not your favorite person."

"Nonsense, you're a valued customer of our bank. Your presence is always welcome."

Spoken like a true businessman. I knew, as well as he did, it was only my business that made me welcome. "Nevertheless, thank you."

"Thank you for helping my father."

"Of course. Please send him my wishes for a speedy recovery."

He nodded and returned his attention to his work. I closed the door behind me as I left. Kelsey and Pete were waiting for me in the lobby. "How'd it go?"

The nervousness in her voice prompted me to smile in reassurance. "Depends. Have either of you heard about the Diamantes?"

Kelsey's face scrunched in confusion, but Pete's registered a measure of alarm. "Let's go to Kelsey's office," he suggested.

Once in the room, he shut the door. Kelsey couldn't take it one more second, based on the anxious look she wore. "Pete, what's going on?"

He gestured to the chairs. "Let's sit down."

We obliged, then looked at him expectantly. He exhaled slowly. "I've only heard whispers, but these are powerful people." He directed his full attention to me. "People who should not be messed with."

"It's truly not my intention to mess with anyone, but I'm getting the distinct impression they're trying to mess with me, or, more aptly, my family."

"Any idea why?"

"I'm beginning to think JB's meeting with Sydney gave them an opportunity. I don't know if that's still the case or if they're now worried about what he might have shared with her"

"Which is what?" Pete rejoined the conversation.

"Pete!"

"No, it's okay. If I share, maybe you can help me figure out my next step."

Pete reached over and took Kelsey's hand with a smile before returning his attention to me. "You know you can count on us."

I believed him. I shared with him about the batteries and JB's belief that CellCo was behind their improper disposal. I hesitated only a moment before continuing. "There's one more thing but I can't be certain if it is connected or not."

"Let's hear it," Kelsey encouraged. "If it's irrelevant, we'll move on."

This was a pivotal moment for me personally. Learning to trust and share, at least with those outside of my team, had been a difficult transition. I recalled hearing the pain in Kelsey's voice when she'd learned about my sister, just one of many details I'd kept from not only her but everyone. She, however, wasn't just anyone. Wanting to prove I was changing, I nodded. "I also believe JB put some information in the materials that were provided to Sydney. Information I don't think they wanted her to have."

"What kind of information?" Kelsey leaned forward, fully in the moment with me.

"There was a clipping from Emerson's parents about the story they were going to break about CellCo. According to Isabella, shortly after the article came the boating *accident*..." I resorted to the air quotes again to further make my point. "Their research was never found, and the story was dropped."

"Someone high up had to kill that story. Even if the Romanos kept everything close to the vest, I can't believe the paper would just move on. Journalists thrive on getting the truth out."

Pete was right. "Who was the editor-in-chief at the time of their deaths?"

"Chester McAllister," Kelsey supplied.

"Is his family connected or high enough on the social food chain to be part of the Diamantes?"

Kelsey shook her head. "I wouldn't think so."

I sighed, disappointed in another potential dead end. Before I could wallow in pity too long, Kelsey continued. "But the owner of the paper is."

An image formed in my brain, one boasting several pictures with yarn connecting them like one would see on the murder boards in crime dramas. I needed to see this outside my head. "Can I borrow a piece of paper?"

Kelsey handed me a legal pad and pen. I started writing names. "Okay, obviously the Birmingham family is in the secret club along with the McIntyres. What family owns the paper?"

"The Devlyn family."

Now that name I'd heard before. "As in Jason Devlyn?"

"Well, his father, Michael. Besides the paper, he owns multiple media outlets."

"I'm going to circle back to them, but first I want to know if there are any other families you think might be a part of this network?"

"The Cutter family."

I'd heard that name before. "That's not surprising. They're pretty high on the social food chain as well." Thinking of a couple of the families and the drama surrounding them, I added, "I'm sure the Cutters and McIntyres' children have given the Diamantes some cause for concern in recent years." They'd both been in trouble with the law. Now that I considered it further, the news coverage on their problems had been minimal. Perhaps it was the work of Michael Devlyn, controlling the press and other news outlets?

Kelsey chuckled, "Yes, apparently, untold wealth doesn't mean you have class and morals."

"Tell 'em, babe," Pete chimed in with an approving smile.

I graced them both with a grin. "Okay, let's circle back to the Devlyns. Is Michael involved in anything besides his media empire?"

"He has other what I'd call rich people roles. You know, running charities, sitting on boards..." Pete had opened the door and expected me to walk through it.

"Michael Devlyn sits on the board of CellCo?"

"He does," Pete confirmed.

This would require more processing. Lester had been seen with Jason Devlyn. Jason was someone Jackie told me one wouldn't want to know, but that Lester had no choice. "What about his son? What or who does he work for?"

Kelsey sat back in her chair and folded her hands. "That's a really good question. No one is entirely sure. His earlier career aspiration to become a law enforcement officer didn't work out. No one really asks or questions why he failed or what he does now. His family has the kind of money that doesn't require a day job."

Pete continued. "He keeps a pretty low profile. You rarely see him in socials or press about his family. Which makes me wonder how you know about him."

"I saw him at the marina the other day with Lester. The two left together."

"Oh, that's not good," Kelsey muttered.

"Why not? I mean, Jackie said he didn't really have a choice, but she didn't offer up much more explanation."

"There are just rumors that if Jason comes to visit you, it's never a good thing."

Great, more general information that had very little context. Maybe flunking out of being a cop had made him go to the dark side? I scribbled a few notes, including a reminder for myself to check in with Jess to see if she had been able to uncover any dirt on him. "Okay, so we have the Birminghams, McIntyres, Cutters, and Devlyns. Anyone else?"

"The Jacobs family," Kelsey shared, but the look on her face told me there was something more about this name.

"Never heard of them."

"No, but you know their daughter. You just know her by her married name."

"Who?"

Pete rubbed his forehead and chuckled, "You're not going to like the answer."

"Just tell me." The suspense was sending my pulse skyrocketing again. I'd had enough adrenaline for one day.

"Karen Bizzy."

Chapter Twelve

Of all the people I didn't want to go talk to today, Karen Bizzy was in the top five. Heck, maybe even the top three. Dora Lee had the coveted top position.

Honestly, how could a mother not let her son know his father had a heart attack?

Not wanting to let myself spend too much time on that thought, I stood and sighed, "Then, I guess she's my next stop."

Pete and Kelsey stood as well. Pete shook his head. "I don't expect she'll know much. This is more of good ol' boys club, if there ever was one."

I'd just used this same term, but I couldn't leave this stone unturned. "Can't hurt to ask."

"Please be careful," Kelsey offered with a concerned look.

"Careful is my middle name."

"Ha!" She laughed, "I'm pretty sure it's Anne."

My gaze snapped to hers. I didn't care that she knew my middle name, but I did care how she'd obtained the information. While I didn't mind Kelsey knowing more about me, my personal details were not to be privy for the whole world to see.

She interpreted my look accurately. "Relax. When I entered the forms for your investments, we had to use your legal name. You only put A, so I guessed and the system confirmed it matched government records."

Guess the government really did know everything. "Sorry, I know it's not a big deal, I just–"

"Value your privacy. I get it. Our records are safeguarded and kept under lock and key, along with being encrypted. Your secret is safe." She winked.

"Thanks for understanding."

I was getting ready to head over to Karen's when I realized it was the middle of the day and Pete wasn't at work. "Hey, shouldn't you be at the office?"

Pete chuckled. "Maybe I wanted to see what it would be like not to have a day job."

"Nice try. No way would Kelsey agree to be your Sugar Momma."

They both laughed at that. Pete slipped his arm around Kelsey's shoulders. "Ah, c'mon, babe. You know I've always wanted to be a kept man."

"And I've always wanted to be a trophy wife. Guess neither of us gets what we want," she teased back.

"Well, then I guess the fact I took some comp time after working nights and weekends on this latest case will have to be the explanation."

"Sounds more believable. Enjoy your day."

Pete's smile faded. "Hey, aren't you going to ask me about the case?"

I suppose that was fair since I was typically very inquisitive. "Does it have to do with the current drama in my life? If not, I can save my questions for later."

"I don't know if it's directly related, but I think you should know."

He certainly had my attention. "And you're just going to tell me? I don't have to bribe you or provide reassurances about not inadvertently sharing the information?" Pete's intel usually came with stipulations.

He looked at his watch. "No, since the paperwork has now officially been filed. It's a matter of public record."

"Does this have something to do with CellCo?" I asked. Pete understood, to some extent, how my mind worked. If he thought I should know, then it was related.

"FES filed a formal suit today in civil court claiming CellCo committed corporate espionage when they stole the plans for the solid-state batteries."

"Allegedly," I teased. "C'mon, Pete, we still live in an innocent until proven guilty country." Though, with Carmen receiving the proof less than fifteen minutes before JB was killed, this was no laughing matter.

"It's cute you believe that," he retorted with a smile. "The government denied CellCo's request for a grant and a few months later, right after a break-in at Future Energy Sources research and development lab, they announced potential contracts for the sale of those batteries. It doesn't take a math genius to figure out they had help."

He wasn't wrong. Wanting to provide full disclosure, I added, "Their head of research being handed a smoking gun was likely the help they needed to prove their case."

Pete's gaze widened and snapped to mine. After a moment, he shook his head. "I shouldn't be surprised you knew about that. Dare I ask how?"

"I'll tell you over some tequila after all of this is over. Too long to explain right now."

Pete nodded. "Fair enough. They're as dirty as it comes, so it's high time someone can prove it. Personally, I'm glad it's my firm that will put the nails in their coffin."

Sadly, it was more JB's bravery and sacrifice that ultimately would be the catalyst for CellCo's fall from grace. Which meant I needed to find out who killed him, not just to clear Sydney's name but to ensure his efforts were not in vain. "I agree about them being dirty. I think the president of their board has been trying to drive them through all this mud."

"That will be harder to prove, but Scott McIntyre is certainly a force of nature when it comes to getting what he or a company he represents wants."

Pete and I could probably talk about this all day, but I needed to get moving. This was supposed to be my last stop, but now I would need to visit Karen to ask about her father. "Let's talk more about this later. But Pete..."

"Yes?"

"You were right," I offered with a smile.

He laughed. "I'm always right, but it's nice to hear it. What was I right about?"

"I did need to know. There's a lot going on around here, and my gut tells me CellCo is at the center of it–at least the majority of it." I couldn't tie them to the drugs, but they were the number one suspect for the corporate espionage, JB's death, and, most likely, the death of Emerson's parents.

I believed it, but now I needed to prove it.

"Please be careful, Sadie," Kelsey warned as she came over to give me a hug. "Call if you need anything, even if it's just to talk."

Returning her hug, I squeezed a little tighter. "I will."

Waving goodbye to Pete and Kelsey, I headed to my truck. I sent a quick text to Sydney to let her know I should be home soon. From my burner phone, I called Jackie Price.

"What?" she answered with a growl.

I thought about being sassy and extra cheery, but I knew she was worried about Lester, as was I, and no one had time for games today. "Any news on Lester?" I figured I'd start with what was most important to her before I asked her anything more.

"No."

Maybe she'd been hanging around One-Word Richard and picked up on his habits. "I've not forgotten about him, I promise."

"What do you want?"

Okay, so maybe she hadn't spent enough time around Richard just yet. Since she wanted to be direct, I got straight to the point. "I need Karen's number."

"Why?"

"I need to talk to her."

There was a long pause. "Not happening."

I remembered my mom talking about some doctors at the VA hospital making her "hackles rise." While I couldn't be entirely sure what a hackle was, there was a good chance mine were rising at this very moment. "What's not happening? You giving me her number, or me talking to her?"

"You're not getting her number."

This woman was unbelievable. Had she already forgotten the number of bullets that had narrowly missed me while trying to save her brother? And all I was asking for was a lousy number. Thankfully, all those thoughts were inside my head rather than spoken out loud. I tried to remember the last time I'd eaten. Maybe I was getting hangry (irrationally angry because I was so hungry). Instead, I managed a one-word response of my own that spoke volumes. "Fine."

I hung up and headed toward Karen's house. I might not have her number, but I knew where she lived. On the short drive over, I checked my non-burner phone. Sydney hadn't read my text yet. She was probably hanging out with a hot shower for a while. I couldn't blame her. I'd want to wash off being around Detective Matthews as much as possible, too. Oh yeah, I was definitely hangry. Maybe after seeing Karen, I could grab Sydney and we'd get something to eat before the appointment with JT this afternoon.

Richard and Karen Bizzy's house was not hard to find when one knew what to look for. A brick home surrounded by a privacy fence so tall it would ward off even the most innovative paparazzi. According to local buzz, the fence went up soon after the RV park went in across the street. Karen's aversion to *normal* people had been a source of contention between us from the very beginning. We'd had temporary truces from time to time. I hoped this would be one of those instances.

While I plotted how to approach her, my phone started blaring. Quickly unlocking it, I realized it was the security alarm at my house. The camera feed revealed the front door had been breached. Immediately, I put the truck in gear and sent my foot to the floor. The chances of me getting home in time were slim, but I had to try. I hit record on the feed in the hope I'd capture something that would help me identify later who dared to violate my private sanctum.

My foot pushed the gas pedal all the way down when I saw two men dragging Sydney out the front door. My heart lurched into my throat. She was putting up a good fight, but she was no match for the muscled men.

I heard a voice yelling, "Let her go, you bullies!"

It was my next-door neighbor, Jerry. A moment later, he entered the vision field of the camera. He was brandishing a gun. The men paid him no attention and continued to drag Sydney, kicking and screaming, down my front steps.

"Release her or I'm going to shoot you!"

A tall, thin man emerged from the house at the threat. Without hesitation, he pulled a gun and aimed it toward Jerry. Though I couldn't hear the shot due to a silencer on the barrel of the gun, my heart stopped beating as Jerry rolled to the ground. At the same time, the men shoved Sydney into the back of a pickup truck that looked eerily the same as the one that gave Lester his unscheduled Uber drive.

And just like that, she was gone.

Chapter Thirteen

I drove like a bat out of Hades, trying to get to the house as fast as I could. I was about to call 911 when the truck I believed to be holding Sydney sped by me on the opposite side of the road. I swung around in my seat and used the camera on my phone to snap a picture of the license plate before making an illegal U-turn to give chase.

The fact that there was only one road in and out of Wilson worked to my advantage. Within a minute, I was hot on their tail. I hit send on the 911 call and reported the abduction, relaying what I could remember about the men, the make and model of the truck, along with their license plate number. I also reported about Jerry being shot.

While the operator did what she does, I put the phone on speaker and concentrated on following the truck. The back window of their getaway vehicle opened and someone stuck his hand out with one finger up. Not that one, the index finger. He wagged it back and forth in the universally understood sign of, "No, no, no." Then, he pulled Sydney where I could see her and put the gun to her head.

Message received.

I eased off the accelerator. They held all the advantages now. Tears clouded my vision as the distance between me and my twin sister grew greater and greater. Pulling off the road, I allowed myself a moment to feel all my emotions. I closed my eyes and willed Sydney to feel my support reaching out to her across the distance, followed by my promise that I would find her.

Find her and make the men who'd messed with my family pay.

I arrived in front of my house a few minutes later. The paramedics had arrived, and the vice grip around my chest eased a bit when I saw Jerry sitting up and arguing with the EMTs. "Jerry! Are you all right? I saw them shoot you!"

He waved off my concern. "You saw them shoot *at* me. I did a quick dive, making the bullet barely graze me."

"Do you think he missed on purpose?" Typically, people who were going to commit an abduction in broad daylight would know how to use the guns they brought.

"Ha!" Jerry scoffed. "You think that's the first time I've been shot at?"

As a matter of fact I did, but I wasn't going to admit it. He laughed at my non-response. "Muscle memory from all those years in taekwondo."

I didn't doubt the muscle memory part, but I wondered if it was from martial arts training or his time in the military. I was grateful either way. "So, just a little scratch?"

The EMT rolled his eyes as he applied a gauze bandage to his arm. "This is more than a graze. You're going to need stitches."

"I'll be fine. You worry about yourself." After scolding the EMT, he returned his attention to me. "You, on the other hand, need to worry about your sister. You get a plate or description of those idiots who took her?"

"Yes, I got the plate. Already reported it to the police. And I only have the basics of the description of the men, but I have camera feed saved that will hopefully help."

"Good."

The 911 operator butted into the conversation. Honestly, I'd forgotten she was there. "Ma'am, we've issued an APB on the license plate and vehicle you called in about and notified local law enforcement and paramedics about the shooting. Are they on scene?"

"Yes, ma'am. Thank you."

"Do you require further assistance from me?"

"No, ma'am."

As soon as I hung up, my least favorite local law enforcement officer showed up. "Everyone all right?"

Jerry saved me from having to answer. "I'm fine, but they nabbed Sydney."

I could have been wrong, but Deputy Jake Matthews looked more concerned than I'd ever seen him. "Any idea who?"

"Uncertain," I answered with a frown.

He nodded. "Emergency Services brought me up to speed. You have any footage from those fancy cameras of yours?"

Quickly, I downloaded the footage and transferred the file over to his phone. "All right, gimme a minute to look at it to see if I recognize anyone."

I had zero explanation for why he was so pleasant, but a small measure of gratitude filled my worried heart. It was probably because Sydney had charmed him. She did mention they'd gotten along great while she was being held. For her, I would put aside my dislike for him and strive for cooperation.

"Let me look at that with you. Everything happened so fast, I can't be sure if I've seen them before or not." Jerry moved over to stand next to him.

Deputy Jake nodded. "Sounds good."

While they reviewed the footage, I stepped a few feet away to call Jess. "Hey, I'm sorry to call you on an unsecured line, but the situation has become critical. My sister has been abducted. I'm sending you the footage from my security camera and the license plate number of the truck they drove."

"I'm on it, Sadie. I'm still wading through everything, but I've learned enough to know CellCo is bad news. They were relatively quiet and not in the news until a little over five years ago. Then, articles started showing up alleging all was not right."

"Any idea what the catalyst was for the change?"

"I haven't been able to find anything yet that would wield enough influence to cause that shift."

I paused as my brain worked through all the knowledge I'd gained working cons over the past couple decades. Who in an organization had the power to affect that kind of change? It had to come from the top. CEO, CFO, or any of the three-letter acronym positions could potentially do it. And...the board. But not just anyone on the board, it would have to be the most influential member: the president. "Check to see when Scott McIntyre became part of the board and when he became president. Then, cross reference with whatever internal changes you can dig up and the timeline for when they started getting bad press." With the articles in the brown folder I'd recovered from Sydney's rental, I could probably do it, but a computer was faster. And Jess was the best at this kind of thing.

"I'm on it, boss. I'm also closing in on those deleted files. Be in touch soon."

She hung up before I could remind her that I wasn't her boss anymore, but I figured old habits died hard. My next call was going to be to Jeremy. Before I could dial his number, my phone rang and my knight in khaki armor was calling me. "Hey."

"Hey, Sadie."

"I was just going to call you."

"What's wrong?"

Everything. "Why does something have to be wrong for me to call you?"

"Because you know I'm at work and you wouldn't call me while I was here unless something was wrong."

"The way you get me is sweet and a little disconcerting. I'll try to be less predictable."

He chuckled. "Oh, don't worry, you're still a pretty big mystery."

I wasn't sure if that was a good thing or not. Avoiding the subject any further, I started to tell him about Sydney. Before I could say anything, he shared, "I have news on the Big D cartel."

I'd tell him about Sydney right after his news. I was convinced it was all connected...somehow. "What did you learn?"

"They moved into this area about six months ago and immediately began to eliminate the rival gangs and dealers. There really weren't many, and it was a quick transition of power. They're ruthless, as you would expect from an organized cartel."

"Agreed. Is it their drugs or the increased presence resulting in the deaths?"

"Could be both, but I learned from my contact that their drugs are cut with synthetic cannabinoids, which make them more potent and potentially harmful outside of normal drug side effects. Ingesting these drugs can lead to paranoia and serious respiratory issues."

My blood pressure was rising quickly. Sydney could be with these dangerous men. "I want to know more, but..."

He continued. "You're wondering what synthetic cannabinoids are, aren't you?"

It was a valid question. "Yes, that would be good to know." Reasonably, I knew it had something to do with cannabis, but my brain was spinning with possibilities.

"From what he shared, the primary source is THC vape cartridges."

I had a million questions, but my worry over Sydney was keeping me from being able to focus. When I didn't say anything after he revealed this detail, he said my name in a way that cut through the madness for just a moment. "Sadie, what's wrong?"

I inhaled and exhaled slowly for composure and to not cry. I was *not* going to let Detective Matthews of all people see me lose my composure. "Sydney's been kidnapped."

"Lead with that, Sadie. That's more time sensitive than my intel." The anxiety in his voice was evident.

"I was going to, but your information could help us find her. I don't know if it's the cartel that has her, but my gut thinks they're connected somehow."

"The police are there?"

"Yes, they abducted her in broad daylight. I have camera footage. Detective Matthews and my neighbor are reviewing it now."

"They're going to find her."

Or I would. "I have faith."

After a few moments, I refocused. What I needed to do now to help Sydney was learn all I could about this cartel and, if they were responsible for kidnapping her and all this other mayhem Jeremy had shared, I would find a way to make them pay. I repeated my mantra: No one messed with my family.

Resuming the conversation, I asked, "Distract me for a few minutes while I'm waiting on them to review the footage. I know vaping is popular, but THC is still illegal in most states. I'm confident it is in Texas. Since that's the case, where do they source them from?"

"Okay, I'll distract you with information for a few minutes, but then we're circling back to Sydney."

"Deal."

"Our proximity to the border suggests that they're bringing it in from our neighbor to the south."

Working to slow the scenarios spinning through my head, I inhaled, held my breath for a few seconds, and then slowly let the air out. "Are there states the cartridges are legal in?"

He was silent for a moment. "New Mexico is probably the closest."

While I couldn't be sure where the sources in Mexico were, it was reasonable to assume there might be places they could obtain them closer than the thirteen to fourteen hours it would take to get them from New Mexico. Though, I guessed that the option of a private plane would be available as well. An established cartel would have access to all modes of travel. I also remembered Jackie mentioning Lester's trip he took not too long ago to New Mexico. It could be a coincidence, but I wasn't a big fan of those. It also made me wonder if the diamonds Lester had been hiding for the cartel was payment for these cartridges rather than drugs, as I'd originally thought. That would make the most sense given the information I now had.

"Sadie, are you still there?" Jeremy's deep voice cut into my scattered brain.

"Yes, just processing the new information. Anything else you can tell me? Who are the major players?"

"Real names aren't known. My contact simply referred to them as Big D and Little D. They believe it's a father and son team."

Memories from my time at Flying V Campground flooded into the forefront of my mind. I could remember him mentioning his father. Was that just a coincidence, or was the man making the threats against Lester none other than the head of the Big D Cartel? "I think you're right, and I feel it in my gut they now have Lester and Sydney."

"I'll be there as soon as I can," Jeremy started.

"I appreciate it, but I'm not sure what you can do here."

Jeremy didn't hesitate. "My main goal would be to make sure you don't go all Lone Ranger and try to bring the cartel down yourself."

Though I should have been upset at his insinuation that I needed to be looked after or reined in, I admit my heart melted a little at his thoughtfulness. Honestly, I didn't want to be alone right now. "Um, hello, I would be going all Wonder Woman on them. I'd love to have you here, but..."

"No buts. I'm headed your way. Please don't do anything until I get there."

"I'll do my best. And Jeremy?"

"Yes?"

"Thank you."

"You're welcome." I could almost hear the smile in his voice as we disconnected the call.

Deputy Matthews interrupted my happy respite with an, "Oh my God!"

"What is it?" He gestured me over and pointed to his screen. He'd frozen the frame and zoomed in on the man who shot at Jerry, the color fading from his normally ruddy complexion.

"This man. I know him. His picture is on our Wall to Watch."

Any respite I'd felt after speaking with Jeremy dissipated like smoke from a dying fire. I blinked to focus on the thin, well-dressed man. My color faded as well. "I know who that is, too."

"Well, who in the devil is it?" Jerry chimed in with more than a little aggravation.

"It's Jason Devlyn."

Chapter Fourteen

Detective Matthews and I had responded at the same time. I wasn't sure I liked being in sync with him, but I'd roll with it for now.

"No idea who that is," Jerry shared. It might have been the first time I'd heard him admit to not knowing something about anything.

Detective Matthews jumped in. "We're pretty sure he's bad news. He's always around trouble, but we can never pin anything on him. He's as slippery as they come."

"Everyone I've talked to about him says the same thing." I looked at Jake. "What's our next move?"

He shook his head. "You need to stay here and let us do our jobs."

It was like the man just met me. "Look, I get where you're coming from, but they have my sister. I can't just sit around waiting for a call." I sensed our temporary truce on Sydney's behalf was about to come to an end.

"Don't make me use resources to babysit you to make sure you dang well do what you're told."

Ah, now that's the Jake Matthews I knew and didn't love. "Fine, I'll wait for your call."

The look of surprise on Jerry's face was worth the look of satisfaction on the deputy's. "That's a good girl. I'll let you know as soon as I know something."

My tongue was almost bleeding from not offering a scathing retort. *Good girl?* He'd poked the bear–no, make that the tiger–and the moment he was out of my line of vision, I was going to do something. It had been decades since anyone had referred to me as their good girl, and that included my father.

He drove off, and Jerry started chuckling.

I had to know. "What's so funny?"

"That boy is about as dumb as a newborn donkey."

"Well, he certainly is a jack–"

"As you were saying to the man on the phone," Jerry interrupted me. "You're going to wait for him, right?"

I shook my head. "I'm going to go visit Karen Bizzy. Maybe she can provide answers or at least give me some direction. That's where I was when all of this started." Seeing the look of disapproval on Jerry's face, I amended my statement. "I'll call Jeremy to let him know where I am. You going to be okay?"

"Nothing a little red wine won't fix."

Oh, the beauty of self-medication. "Well, if it starts to do more than annoy you, please call me or the EMTs. I'd never forgive myself if anything happened to you."

"Save all that mother-henning for your sister. Now, go on, time to save the world."

I pulled him into a quick hug, even though I knew he'd fuss. "This time, I'm just trying to save my sister."

"And Lester, too?"

I offered a dramatic sigh. "Yeah, him, too."

"I'll call someone to come fix your door."

"Thanks, Jerry. For everything."

He waved off my thanks and turned toward his home. I got in the truck and headed to Karen Bizzy's fortress. The garage door was up when I arrived. I maneuvered my vehicle to block any exit she might try to make. Jumping out, I offered a smile. "Hey, Karen."

"Oh hey, Sadie. No time to chat, somewhere to be."

"This won't take long. I need your help."

"Quickly then."

Quick suited me just fine. I didn't have time to waste. "What do you know about the Diamantes or Jason Devlyn?"

"I'm not sure why you'd think I'd know anything about either one of those things." She cast a glance back at her house. I was sure she was wondering if Richard would come to her rescue. *Not today, Karen. Not today.*

"Because I believe your father is a Diamante and the messed-up sense of loyalty and protecting each other's backs has relentlessly covered up a multitude of sins including, I believe, murder."

She stepped closer to me. "Are you accusing my daddy of murder?"

Maybe. "No, but he might know who orchestrated it. Jason Devlyn is looking more and more guilty by the minute."

"Oh, please. I've known Jason his whole life. He doesn't have the gumption to plan a murder. Besides, the last I heard he was doing odd jobs for his father's friends to get back on the good side of everyone."

There was a lot to unpack in that statement. I started with, "Why isn't he on his father's good side?"

The withering look she sent me would've made lesser women cry, I'm sure. "Seriously? He defied his father by wanting to become a cop instead of taking his place as the heir to the media throne, and then he flunks out? I can't imagine the humiliation his father must've felt."

Never mind how that would've made Jason feel, I thought. "Wouldn't that have made his father happy? I get failure is a disappointment to anyone, but this meant Jason would be ready to take his rightful place in the family business."

Richard came out to join his wife. "Okay?" he asked Karen, giving me the side eye. He didn't trust me much, but that didn't bother me. The man only spoke one word at a time. How bad could he really diss me?

"I'm good, honey. Just schooling Sadie on how father and son relationships work."

"Why?"

Karen laughed, "Because she asked."

He looked at me with confusion, which prompted me to explain. "More like I asked about the Diamantes, the super-secret elite club a lot of fathers are in, including your wife's. She then shared about Michael and Jason Devlyn."

My sharing appeared to ease his mind. He nodded. "Trouble."

"Agreed. Jason has been around every time something bad has happened recently."

Richard looked like he was about to say something, but Karen cut him off. "Thanks for checking on me, sweetheart. Once Sadie and I finish up, I'm headed to the store. Let me know if you need anything not already on the list."

"Okay." He gave me one last look before heading inside. I wasn't sure if he was attempting non-verbal communication or levying a final warning about irritating Karen. Either one was possible.

"Anything else?" Karen's impatience started to show, not that she'd shown anything else to me...ever.

I sighed, "Karen, both Lester and my sister have been taken by men I believe to be part of the Big D Cartel. Jason Devlyn was at my sister's abduction a short time ago, and he shot Jerry."

"He shot someone?" Her gaze widened in disbelief.

"Technically, he shot at my neighbor. Thankfully, he was able to do some fancy martial arts stuff and avoid a significant impact. There's no reason he won't make a full recovery. Why is that so shocking? I mean, he's on the Sheriff's Wall to Watch, everyone I've talked to says he's bad news, and even Jackie thinks when he comes to visit, it's not good."

"I guess you're right," she sighed heavily. "It's just, knowing him as long as I have, I can't believe he's so far gone down the wrong path. I get he was angry from failing out of the academy, but to shoot someone? That's a whole other level."

I wasn't sure what to say, but I wanted to offer some explanation. "Sometimes, the company we keep can influence us more than we realize because they chip away at who we are a little at a time. Before we know it, we've become a whole different person. If he's been hanging out with criminals and the cartel, it wouldn't take long before those lines between who he was and who he's become are blurred so much they're hard to see."

"I guess you're right."

"Is there anything you can or will tell me?" It was a last ditch effort to build on the common ground we'd found.

Her gaze found mine, those dark eyes holding me, and I waited to see what she'd say.

"Look, it's a boys' club. Girls aren't allowed as far as I've been able to tell. My father hit the chromosome trifecta as he fathered three girls and no sons. I overheard him tell my mother at a family dinner recently he was glad his oath would die with him. He only wanted to preserve the Texas way of life. Now, he's at the beck and call to promote the agenda of someone who is more interested in self-promotion and his own legacy than anything of benefit to the state."

"Why don't the rest of the members tell this one guy where to get off?"

She shook her head slowly. "It doesn't work like that. For better or worse, these men swore an oath to help each other. They take that very seriously."

I could have argued that when the mandate changed, the condition of their oath would've changed, too, but there was no time and I simply didn't have the energy. "Do you know who the problem member is?"

"No."

"Any idea where or if they meet?"

"No."

"Okay, then I think we're done."

Karen didn't say anything, just crossed her arms and waited for me to move my truck. With nothing more to gain than being further stonewalled, I left and returned to my house. Jeremy was waiting for me.

"I thought you agreed to wait," he questioned as he opened my door for me.

"I agreed to not go all Wonder Woman on them before you got here. I visited Karen Bizzy. That wasn't even Super Girl level danger."

He laughed. "Okay, so what's next?"

"Let's go inside. I need to talk through everything and write it down so I know what's next."

He held up a sack. "I brought takeout from that little Italian bistro you like. Didn't want you getting hangry."

I should have asked him to marry me right then and there. Instead, I offered, "Thank you. That was very thoughtful."

Once inside, I noticed there was very little disruption to the interior of my home given someone had just been abducted from here. Sydney was certainly kicking and resisting once she got outside. Maybe that was for the benefit of my camera?

Jeremy brought me a plate of food and we sat at the table. I pulled out my notes but decided to start fresh. "Okay, let's try to organize all of this. Given the threads we've been trying to tie together, we have two to four timelines to work through."

He nodded, his mouth full of food. "Mmmhmm."

So very adorable. Focus, Sadie! "All right, I'm going to make notes, then we can talk about them."

Starting with a blank piece of paper, I sorted my thoughts and knowledge:

JB was a whistleblower on CellCo

1 Corporate Espionage

2 Battery Disposal

3 Romano death?

Corporate espionage - JB delivered proof to Carmen of FES Friday night, only ten to fifteen minutes before his murder. Carmen delivered that proof to her attorneys, and they filed suit on Monday.

Battery disposal: JB met with Sydney early Friday evening. Meeting witnessed by Robert and EZ. Suspect Scott

McIntyre sent them (well, Robert and he made him take EZ, maybe for leverage later?)

JB met Sydney at the lighthouse but said there were too many eyes so they agreed to meet later. She was to rent a boat. He would give her a date/time but never did. Why? Waiting to hear from Carmen first? Changed his mind?

I chewed on the tip of my pen as I thought about this for a moment. Jeremy interrupted my train of thought. "There's perfectly good food right there in front of you. No need to eat your pen."

I smiled but kept my focus. Sydney was out there and needed my help. I wasn't going to stop to eat, no matter how sweet the gesture was. "What time did the fire break out on Friday?"

"We think it was late afternoon. By early evening, it was blazing and filling the air with smoke."

"Could the flames be seen from The Flying V?"

"Depends on the time. It's possible. Why do you ask?" He put his fork down and concentrated on my questions.

"Because we now know the batteries were the cause of the fire. Even if JB saw the smoke and flames, he must not have realized the batteries were the source. Once at the lighthouse, he would've known that area was unavailable to him even if the batteries hadn't been affected."

"Maybe that's why he asked her to meet him later?"

"Sydney told me there were too many eyes on them. Initially, I thought it was him worried about the people he believed were after him, but now I'm thinking it was probably the patrols around the area of the fire. He wouldn't have been able to get in there to show her proof."

"True, he might have thought the fire would be contained later that night, or maybe he was just going to tell her to wait for the fire marshal's report once he realized it was going to take a while for the blaze to be contained."

This was good. I felt like we were making some progress, even if we were simply developing our own narrative with the details we knew. Had to start somewhere. "Okay, thank you. That was helpful."

Jeremy nodded and smiled and went back to his food. I went back to my notes.

JB is murdered Friday night. Sometime Saturday, Lester falsely IDs Sydney/me. Sydney is held for questioning. If CellCo is behind it, what's Lester's motivation to get involved?

"Didn't your mother teach you that your face could get stuck like that?" Jeremy offered the tease with a small smile.

"Oh, I guess I'm concentrating too hard. I need to figure this out for Sydney."

He moved over to sit beside me and pulled me into a hug, "Hey, I'm sorry. I'm trying to distract you, but I understand, that's not what you need right now."

"Normally, I'd be game for a distraction."

"But now we need to find your sister," he finished for me.

"Yes."

"Okay, so what has your beautiful face scrunched up in confusion?"

"We know Lester gave the false ID to the police. He thought it was me, but regardless, I know he didn't see the shooting, at least not from the marina. How did he know, then? Or who told him?"

Jeremy kept one arm over my shoulder as he contemplated my question. Maybe JB told him he met Sydney."

I remembered Kelsey sharing that JB and Lester had been at happy hour on Friday night, looking less than happy. "Maybe. Why would Lester care, though? Even if he thought it was me?"

We pondered that in silence until a thought hit me. "The diamonds and batteries were basically in the same part of the lake. My favorite little cove."

"Okay..." Jeremy drew out the word trying to make sense of it all.

"When I spoke with Jackie earlier, she and I both agreed that Lester was working for two different bad guys, trying to make the most of his situation. What if bad guy number one is someone at CellCo and bad guy number two is the Big D cartel?"

"You think one of them came to him with the problem and asked him to finger Sydney?"

"It has to be CellCo. Unless JB knew about the diamonds, too."

"Unless Lester told him, I don't see how he could have. It's not like the lake is clear and you can see the bottom."

This made me chuckle. "Very true. I'm even hesitant to swim in it as I have no idea what lurks underneath. But heck, if there are diamonds, maybe I'll take up that hobby."

"The water is safe, but I'm not sure that's a good reason to take up underwater exploring. There's no sunken treasures, except obviously drug cartel property. Kind of risky."

"Fair." I sat for a moment. "We need to find Lester and Sydney and they can just tell us."

"That would be easiest. Any ideas on how to locate them?"

I stood and made my way over to the desk where Sydney had been working on the contents of the brown binder. Before she was abducted. I knelt down to pick up the papers that must have been knocked off in the scuffle. There was a yellow legal pad turned upside down. When I turned it over, I saw scribbled in Sydney's handwriting: "Tag, You're it!"

Since it was totally random, I immediately jumped to the conclusion it had to be a message from Sydney to me. I quickly shuffled through the rest of the papers and looked in the folder. My actions were frantic and hurried.

"Sadie, what's going on?" Jeremy moved to stand next to me as I flung papers everywhere.

"My phone! Where's my phone?"

He immediately retrieved it and returned it to me. I pulled up the app to track the air tag Sydney had placed previously in the folder. I exhaled a long sigh of relief, thankful she'd reactivated it after we spoke. I held it up for his inspection. "I know where to find her."

Chapter Fifteen

Jeremy glanced at the little arrow on my phone. "How?"

"Sydney put an air tag in this folder of information. She was worried someone might try to take it, and she takes protecting her clients and their intel very seriously." I held up the notepad with Sydney's hastily written message. "When she heard them coming in, she must have scribbled this message and put the air tag somewhere on her person. She knew I'd find it and get what she meant."

"Is that a twin thing?" He smiled.

"More like a *we think alike* kinda thing." Not wanting to delay any longer, I grabbed my purse. "You coming?"

"Whoa, hold on a minute. We need to call for backup."

"You call for backup, I'm heading out. You can either come with me or stay." This was a test. I knew it. He knew it. This was me at my core. I put myself in harm's way to protect those I cared about. I would use caution when I got there, but I was going there...now.

To his credit, he only hesitated for a moment. "I'm coming with you AND I'm calling for backup on the way."

"Fair enough. Be sure to tell them no sirens. We can keep them apprised of the situation when we get there." I placed a quick peck on his cheek to let him know how much I appreciated his choice. "Let's go."

Fifteen minutes later, we slowed our approach. Jeremy quietly spoke into his phone to let the law enforcement officers he'd been in contact with since we left Wilson that we were arriving on scene. I heard them caution him, again, to wait for officers to arrive. And, once again, he didn't answer them. He wasn't going to lie, but he also knew there was no way I wasn't going to get a closer look. And he wasn't going to let me do that alone. I admit it was kind of nice having a partner beside me again.

Once out of the truck, we made sure our phones were on silent and screens set to their dimmest level while still allowing me to follow the arrow to Sydney. The place looked abandoned, which concerned me. Maybe they'd found the tracker and left it here to throw us off the trail. Or–a shiver slithered up my spine–she was already dead.

Shaking that gruesome thought, I kept moving forward. I felt the calming presence of Jeremy's hand against the small of my back. Odd how such a small thing could bring my blood pressure down. I turned and offered a smile. His other hand was still holding the phone to his ear, keeping an open line between us and the law. He nodded.

We continued forward, staying next to the buildings as we wove our way to where the bad guys were hiding out. As we turned the next corner, I saw the black truck parked alongside three other vehicles. The license plate, which I'd committed to memory, proved it was the truck. Apparently, the Big D cartel was confident in either their ability to evade or resist arrest since they hadn't bothered to even change the plates on a vehicle involved in two abductions.

Seeing no one, we moved closer, using the vehicles as cover. I didn't see anyone on outside guard duty, but it didn't mean they weren't there. I turned to Jeremy and whispered, "I'm going to get a closer look."

"I'm coming with you."

I shook my head and pointed to the service weapon on his hip. "You're my backup. I need you here to save the day, just in case."

"I can't believe you don't have a gun." His face twisted in a cross between disbelief and concern.

Pulling the pepper spray from my pocket, I admitted the truth. "I get the need for them, but I prefer disabling my opponent and giving them a chance to turn the corner and make amends."

"Honorable, but not practical. We'll discuss it later." He paused, then added, "At a gun range."

Not wanting to argue, I ignored his statement. "You've got my six?"

"One hundred percent."

Moving forward, I kept my head on a swivel and ignored the sweating of my palms. As I knew Sydney, or the air tag, was in the building, I slid the phone into my back pocket. I needed one hand free since the other held my pepper spray.

The windows had blinds, but they were cracked enough I could see in. Lester and Sydney were the guests of honor, tied to chairs in the center of the room. Two guys with guns stood on either side of them. I also noted Don Seymour, Jr., also known as Little D, was watching two others as they bagged up dime bags of drugs as well as a large pile of what I assumed to be the vape cartridges they'd secured, most likely, in the deal for the diamonds on Sunday night.

I was about to return to Jeremy to report on my reconnaissance, when a hand covered my mouth. Rather than try to scream, I simply lifted my hand and depressed the trigger of my pepper spray. The person holding me tightened his grip, but I felt him use his other hand to tend to his eyes. Good luck, buddy. He dragged me to the other side of the building, away from the front door and window. I expected Jeremy to rush to my aid any moment. That was the point of backup, right?

My captor slammed me against the wall and held me there with his forearm across my chest while he continued to scrub at his face. Sadly, I'd missed most of his eyes due to the angle of my approach and, I suspect, him turning his face when he saw it coming. His right eye had received enough to turn it an angry red.

He pulled out a gun and pointed it at my chest. "Stay still!" It was a whispered command, but I heard it loud and clear. The adrenaline continued to surge through my veins, prompting me to fight, but common sense made an appearance in this fight or flight scenario, deciding flight was the better option. As soon as the opportunity presented itself, that was the priority.

With the decision made, I focused on my attacker. I rethought my logic when I realized the gun pointed at me was held by none other than Jason Devlyn. "You killed JB and almost killed Jerry." I was still whispering, but there was conviction in my voice.

"I did not."

"Prove it." A pretty brazen request given my current situation but I figured there wasn't much left to lose. Either Jeremy would rescue me or he wouldn't.

"That's what I'm trying to do."

"By abducting my sister?" I believed that to be a valid question.

He shook his head and chuckled. Seriously, the man was laughing! "You won't believe it, but I took her to protect her."

He was right. I didn't believe him. I trusted my silence conveyed the sentiment. He must've received my message loud and clear as he continued. "They think she has something very important to them. If I let them have her, they would verify the details, one way or the other, and then kill her."

He was speaking in riddles. *They* did have her. Yet, I had to admit, she was still alive. Since I'd been asking this question over the past day or so, I decided to try again. "Who are they?" Maybe this time someone would give me an answer.

"They are–"

Before he could answer, I saw Jeremy standing behind him, gun lifted. A moment later, he hit him on the side of the head with enough force to rotate his head. Jason dropped the gun he was holding on me and fell to the ground.

I looked up at Jeremy. "Seriously?"

His gaze widened. "I'm sure that means thank you in Sadie-speak."

"I was interrogating him, and he was about to give me answers!" I was still whispering, but nearing a normal conversational tone.

This time, Jeremy chuckled. Who knew I was so funny under these circumstances? "Well, pardon me for misreading the situation."

He was right, but I was still frustrated. "Sorry, I know it looked different. Thank you. Since you were rescuing me, what took you so long?"

"I updated the incoming rescue team before moving to the same window you were at to provide a SITREP. Then, I circled around the backside of the building so I could see where you were and what was going on." He looked down at Jason. "I didn't hit him that hard, so we probably have up to fifteen minutes before he regains consciousness. Since you were asking the questions, what did you learn?"

He didn't ask it with a sarcastic tone, but with sincerity. I appreciated that. "He says he didn't kill JB and he abducted Sydney to protect her."

"That makes no sense. Protect her from whom?"

I made a face. "That's what I was about to learn when you knocked him out."

In the dim light from the parking lot light, I could almost see him blush. "Sorry."

"It's okay, always better to rescue me first. Thanks for not shooting him. He will be able to answer more questions when he wakes up."

"Let's be clear, the only reason I didn't shoot him was because it would draw attention to our location."

His logic was sound, even if I didn't agree with it. We'd have to debate that later, over a glass of wine, once Sydney was home safe and the bad guys were behind bars. My smart watch vibrated with an incoming message. Even with my phone on silent, the notifications came through on my wrist. It was from Jess.

The subject of the email was "Must see!" I clicked on the attachment. I realized instantly this had to be the deleted video from the security camera. The footage revealed a boat with three men arriving at the point of Ally's Hangout. One was the driver, and the second man I couldn't see because the third man, who was standing next to him, blocked the view from the angle of the camera. The third man I would have recognized anywhere: Lester Price.

Before I could fully process, the second man raised his arm and fired twice. Lester leaned forward and lost the contents of his stomach. The shooter turned and sat down, apparently unphased from killing JB or Lester's reaction. I couldn't see enough to identify the shooter, but it was apparent his body type didn't match that of Jason's. A moment later, Lester got out of the boat. I couldn't see what he was doing, but he returned in a matter of moments with a shaking of his head. The other men did not appear happy.

"Oh wow," Jeremy whispered.

I'd been so focused on watching, I'd forgotten he was standing next to me. "Did we just witness JB's murder?"

"I'm afraid so."

"Any idea who the shooter was?"

"None, and I'm guessing neither does my colleague or else she would have said. But it does prove one thing."

"What's that?"

I looked to the still unconscious man on the ground. "Jason was telling the truth."

We both pondered the meaning of that for a moment. I was about to say something when a shot rang out. "What the..."

Jeremy and I both peeked around the corner. Standing at the door, arms in the firing position and the pink camo glock gleaming in the artificial light, was Jackie Price. She was rapidly firing and the only thing that kept me from worrying about her inadvertently hitting Sydney was the fact I'd seen her shoot and knew her aim was spot on. That didn't account for the other guys, though.

"Try to wake him up!" I instructed Jeremy while pointing to Jason. "We're going to need his help."

Jeremy shot me a look of disbelief, but knelt beside him. Meanwhile, I leaned forward the smallest bit from my corner of protection. "Jackie!" I whispered loudly, waving my hand from a few feet away. She couldn't hear me from the echo of the gunfire. A moment later, she went down. I couldn't tell if it was a fatal hit or not, but someone dragged her inside and slammed the door.

My heart jumped to my throat, a multitude of emotions swimming through my veins at this development. Not only did I worry for her safety, an additional hostage complicated things even further. Forcing all the negative thoughts to the back corner of my mind, I turned to Jeremy, also noticing that Jason was coming around. "When is backup arriving?"

"Should be soon."

I wasn't sure Sydney, Jackie, and Lester had much more time before the cartel got rid of the evidence, also known as the witnesses, grabbed the goods, and left.

"Let me help you." Jason pleaded with us as he blinked rapidly to clear his head.

"I know you didn't kill JB, but the rest of this is a mystery to me. I'm not sure I can trust you."

"I promise I will explain, but I'm one of the good guys."

I watched his face intently for the slightest expression of deception. I saw none. But my pulse was racing and we were in a potentially life or death situation. My internal lie detector might not have been operating at full capacity. I looked toward Jeremy and arched an eyebrow. A moment later, he answered my unspoken question with a nod.

He turned his attention to Jason. "What's your plan?"

In response, Jason pulled a gun from an ankle holster. To Jeremy's credit, he didn't flinch, but his hand still held his own Glock, ready for action if necessary. "Hide your weapons where you can get to them, but where they can't be seen. I'll pretend I've taken you prisoner. When we get inside, it will be three armed people against three. Little D doesn't usually carry a weapon as he always has his guards with him. The people bagging up the dope aren't armed, either."

"Assuming everyone is safe for the moment, can we try to get them to talk before we start shooting? Dead men don't answer questions."

"I only intend to shoot at the two guys with guns. We need Little D alive."

While I was on board with that plan, I couldn't answer for Jeremy.

"Explain," Jeremy demanded before I could open my mouth.

"We don't really have time for this, but I'm undercover DEA. I've been infiltrating the Big D cartel since they moved into town and took power. Is that enough for you to extend a little trust until we have time for me to explain everything?"

Jeremy nodded. If Jason was lying, he was good at it. Of course, if what he said was true, he was a darn good liar. Everyone believed he was bad, including the cartel. Oh well, decision time. "Let's do this."

Jason handed me a gun. I took it, but I had no intention of using it. Not unless I had no other choice.

"You know how to fire this?" Jeremy asked.

"I do. I just don't want to."

He knew what I meant. "Understood. We get in, get at a good angle. Incapacitate the guys with guns and then rescue the hostages."

Jason nodded. "And I'll need you to knock the gun out of my hand and hold me with Little D. Need to keep the ruse up until we know if he will flip or not."

I didn't like it, but it seemed like a reasonable plan. "Got it. Let's go. I'm not sure how much time we'll have before official help arrives. After that, the narrative is out of our hands."

Jason marched us through the front door. "Look who I found lurking outside," he laughed as he pushed me forward a bit.

"Good Lord, Sadie. You really need to work on your rescues. So far, you're oh for two," Jackie chimed in from the chair next to Lester. I noted her arm had been bandaged, but blood could be seen through the gauze.

With a comment like that, maybe I would shoot her. Nah, just kidding. But I might free her last.

"Quiet!" Little D ordered. He turned his attention to me and then Sydney, before laughing, "I guess ol' Lester was right, there are two of you."

"What's the plan, boss?" Jason asked as he moved to stand next to Jeremy. He still had his gun trained on us. I assumed that was for appearances. The angle now allowed Jeremy the opportunity to make a grab at the weapon.

"Once we get these goodies all bagged up, we call in a cleanup crew. Though," he glared at me and Jackie, "The two of you did a number on my last guys by shooting up their engine block. They're still complaining of injuries. Good thing I found a new, more reliable guy."

"That was me," Jackie shared proudly, and, I thought, stupidly. She shot me another look of disgust. "She would've just pepper sprayed 'em."

Little D laughed. "I like this one, she's got spunk. Be a shame not having her around."

Judging by her wide eyes, I think for the first time, Jackie realized what he meant by the cleanup crew. "Wait, I'm sure we can make some kind of deal."

He ignored her and returned his attention to the packaging of the drugs.

They were almost done. It was time. I elbowed Jeremy, and he looked at Jason. A subtle nod of the head was the cue for the beginning of the end to start. Jeremy grabbed the gun and fired off two quick rounds at the guards. He landed shoulder shots, which knocked the guns out of their hands. I quickly ran to retrieve them while Jeremy turned on Jason and Big D. "Hands in the air. Now!"

I kicked one of the guns away from the two men and grabbed the other to keep it pointed at them with one hand while removing Sydney's restraints with the other. The gun Jason and Jeremy had given me remained tucked at the small of my back. A moment later, another shot rang out, sending everyone ducking. My heart stopped as I heard Jeremy cry out in pain. He fell to the floor.

"No!"

Chapter Sixteen

I fought the urge to run to him. I would have to trust that "soon" should be any minute for the cavalry to arrive. I scanned the room quickly, trying to determine where the shot came from. A moment later, a man emerged from the shadows. He had Jackie's gun. Fan-freaking-tastic. "You can drop your gun, pretty lady."

It only took a moment for recognition to dawn, or at least a reasonable guess. "You're the man who shot JB." It was also a stupid thing to say. Jackie and I could be in a club. I blamed my worry for Jeremy for clouding my judgment.

He laughed. "Your gun. Now."

I complied, at least with the one in my hand.

"Good girl."

That was twice in one day. "I prefer Wonder Woman, but please, go on. Tell us about how you shot JB. Though, I'm more interested in why." Mostly because I already knew how, but there was no need to share that.

"I did my job, plain and simple."

"Not in time, though," Lester piped up for the first time.

"Not my problem that they called me so late. It was bad enough we couldn't make it look like an accident."

"Time for what?" I asked. I figured if help didn't arrive soon, this hired gun–and I was certain now that's what he was– would kill us all, anyway. Might as well get some answers.

"The proof." Lester explained. "JB was handing over evidence of CellCo stealing from FES. I tried to talk him out of it, even refused to lend him a boat." He turned his attention to Little D. "'Cause I know he wanted your diamonds, too."

That must've been another reason JB couldn't take Sydney to see the batteries when they met at the lighthouse. Besides the area crawling with patrols, he didn't have a boat. It was why he'd asked Sydney to rent one.

Lester tilted his head in Sydney's direction. "She must've shown up before we got there. They're gonna wanna talk to her. If she plans on testifying, well, it ain't looking good for her."

If I never heard the word *they* again, it would be too soon. "It wasn't Sydney."

"I saw her on the tape." He smiled. "But I deleted it, so there's no way to prove anything."

The desire to tell him how wrong he truly was hovered on the tip of my tongue. Instead, his sister shot him a look and added, "You really are a moron." She paused, and then softened the jab with a smile. "But, you're my moron."

She must've gotten the *less is more right now* memo, too. I returned my attention to Mr. Hit Man. "Who are the *they* responsible for hiring you to kill JB?"

He took a few steps closer. I didn't retreat. I needed him a whole lot closer before I felt confident about any of my defense tools, even a gun. I hadn't shot one in a very long time. "I'm sure you'd like to know, but I'm not the kinda guy who would kiss and tell." He continued his walk forward.

Jeremy groaned, directing Hit Man's attention away from me. He pointed his gun at him. I needed to stop this. "Wait!"

"I'm just gonna put him out of his misery."

"Since when do you care about suffering? You're a hired gun, for heaven's sake." I was doing anything and everything to distract him. I stepped closer to Sydney, which also brought me closer to him. "Maybe we are the kind of girls who like a man who doesn't kiss and tell." It was lame and it made me sick to my stomach, but desperate times and all.

My plan worked. He forgot about Jeremy and moved in our direction. Sydney's hands were untied, but she'd wisely kept them behind her back when all the chaos broke loose earlier. "Well, now, that is intriguing. I've never had twins before."

I wanted to barf. Instead, I kept my composure. *Just a little closer.*

Sydney realized what I was doing. While crouching down next to her, I put my cheek next to hers and smiled as I slid the pepper spray into her hand. Meanwhile, I used my other hand to retrieve the hidden gun. "Well, we've never had a hit man before, have we, sis?"

If this hadn't been life or death, I would've laughed at her question. But the man was sufficiently distracted by our small talk, which kept him from immediately reacting when I stood and brought the gun to the front, aiming for his center mass. I did this, only because that was the largest target. Not waiting for him to move, I pulled the trigger. The recoil from the shot jerked my hand up and to the right, causing the shot to hit his arm and shoulder area instead. He roared in pain and lunged toward us. I saw Sydney lift the pepper spray, and I darted away from the spray radius. She emptied the contents of the container in the direction of his face.

Sydney moved to stand beside me and I handed her my gun before covering my nose and mouth with my grandfather's handkerchief. Moving closer to the wounded hit man, I landed a solid kick to his groin. It wasn't easy as he was moving around a lot in an effort to tend to his burning, watering eyes. The impact made him forget all about his eyes for a moment. He dropped his gun as his hands moved down to the newly injured area. Once his gun was in my possession, I kept my weapon moving back and forth between all the bad guys. "Free Lester and Jackie," I directed Sydney.

As she moved to comply, I double checked the status of everyone else. They hadn't moved. I had no idea why, but I took this as a small miracle. Kneeling beside Jeremy, I took my gaze off the hostages for only a moment.

It was all it took. I heard footsteps barreling in my direction. Little D must've decided he'd had enough and was going on the offense. Pure instinct kicked in and I raised the gun to shoot. Just as I pulled the trigger, Jason knocked him out of the way and fell to the floor with a thud as my bullet found a home in his body. Ugh! What was he doing?

About that time, the door was breached and the Crockett County Sheriff's deputies, along with some three-letter acronym agencies, came rushing in. The DEA agents went to secure the drug thugs along with Little D and Jason. They called the EMTs in, who tended to Jeremy and Jason. I noticed Lester and Jackie hugging out of the corner of my eye. I grabbed Sydney and hugged her, too.

"Let's go check on your man," Sydney said as she looped her arm through mine. "Wonder Woman," she teased. "I like it."

"More like Wonder Twin powers activated," Jackie said with a smile. "You two made a great team." She put her arm around Lester and hugged him tightly. "Thanks for the rescue, even if it was a bit bumbled. We're gonna need to work on your aim, though."

"Thanks. I'll keep that in mind."

Sydney and I made our way outside, where the EMTs were tending to Jason and Jeremy. I went to my man first. "Hey, how are you holding up?"

"I'll live." He smiled. "Great job in there. Though, I wasn't a fan of your flirting with another man." His statement earned him a smack on the arm. "Ow!"

"That's what you get. I only had to flirt to keep him from shooting you. So, I'll assume that's Jeremy-speak for thank you."

He used his uninjured arm to pull me closer in a kiss that made me forget everyone and everything else going on around us. All too soon, he released me. "Thank you," he smiled.

"My pleasure, especially from that kiss," I added with a wide grin.

"Hey, little sister is in the vicinity. Don't make me tell Mom," Sydney teased.

"Sadie." A hoarse whisper from Jason saved me from responding to my *little* sister.

I squeezed Jeremy's hand. "I'll be right back."

Moving over next to Jason, he motioned me closer and looked around. "Where is Little D?"

"Still inside. The DEA is holding him and the others there."

"Don't sell me out. I'm almost at the finish line. I need all I sacrificed to be worth it."

"Your secret is safe with me. Though, I'd love to hear the rest of the story someday soon."

He nodded. "Maybe someday. I need you to know the cartel wasn't behind the hit. They had no interest in JB unless he was going for the diamonds. You and I both know he wasn't."

"Agreed. Who was behind it, though? All I keep hearing is *they*."

"The Diamantes are my best guess. I don't know exactly who, though."

"Scott McIntyre would be my guess. He has a vested interest in CellCo. I think he ordered the hit on JB and wanted it to happen before he could deliver the proof to Carmen at FES, but he was too late. JB delivered the information to Carmen about ten minutes before he was murdered."

Jason shook his head. "I've been trying to catch them in illegal activities for some time now. Since they thought I was a wash-out, I've been pretending to get in their good graces by doing their dirty work. No one called me."

"Maybe they worried this was too close to home, or maybe they didn't want you to have blood on your hands."

"Maybe."

Our exchange got me thinking. "You intentionally missed Jerry, didn't you?"

Jason smiled. "Yeah, I just wanted to graze him but make it look real. He almost messed it all up with those acrobatics he threw in there."

"Well, he was pretty proud of dodging your bullet, so maybe we'll let him have this one?"

"Deal." Jason coughed and grimaced.

"Sorry about shooting you. I was aiming for Little D."

"I know, but I needed him alive, remember?"

That did ring a bit of a bell. "I do now." There was one more thing I wanted to ask him. "Do you know if CellCo was involved in the death of the Romanos?"

He shook his head. "I remember the story of their deaths. Such a tragedy. I'm not aware, but I'll see what I can find out."

"I'd really appreciate that. Thank you."

"Okay, ma'am, we need to get him to the hospital."

With nothing more to learn from Jason right now, I made my way back to Jeremy. He and Sydney were getting acquainted while the EMTs bandaged his wounds. "You gonna be okay?"

"Yeah, I'm going to live. Though, I might need a personal Florence Nightingale to watch over me for a few days."

Sydney piped up, "I'll call Mom. She's a registered nurse."

I'm sure she thought I would argue, but the thought of having my parents, Sydney, and Jeremy all under the same roof, well, it made my heart burn brightly and long for things I never thought possible. "I think that's a great idea. We'll make the call when we get home."

Jeremy grabbed my hand and squeezed it. "I look forward to spending time with all the Sabatini women."

I leaned in and kissed him. "If you survive that, this relationship has pretty high odds of success, especially if we ever get to have a first date."

He pulled me in for another kiss. Somewhere in the background, I heard Sydney groan, "Ugh, you two, get a room!"

Epilogue

A week later my living room was full. My parents, Sydney, Jeremy, Pete, Kelsey, Emerson, and his aunt were all seated in front of the big screen television.

"Does anyone need anything before it starts?" My mom offered the group.

"Relax, Mom. They've all been fed, have their drinks, and are ready to hear what the six o'clock news is going to say."

"Thank you for offering, Mrs. Delaney," Emerson replied with a smile. It had taken my mom three days to get him to call her that rather than Mrs. Sabatini. I'd tried to warn her he was a proper southern boy through and through, but she was persistent.

"You're welcome, Emerson."

"Shhh, it's starting!" Sydney commanded.

"In our leading story tonight, arrests were made in the murder-for-hire of local businessman and citizen, James Robert Nester, JB to his friends. Mr. Nester had worked at

and served on the board of CellCo for over ten years before uncovering evidence not only of the improper disposal of lithium-ion batteries but also corporate espionage. He delivered the evidence to Carmen DeSantis, her picture shown here, just minutes before he was killed, according to eyewitness testimony and video footage recovered from a nearby security camera.

Michael Devlyn was arrested in connection with the murder. Sources closest to him say he did it to protect his family. This reporter is unsure what that means as his son is currently under arrest for his involvement with the Big D Cartel.

On that story, we have our criminal correspondent, Jazzy Justice."

"Jazzy Justice, really?" My father shook his head.

"I'm sure that's not her real name, Papà," Sydney chimed in.

"Shhh, we can talk after." I gave them both a look. Not a stern one, as I wasn't going to mess with my father, but certainly one indicating my desire to learn all I could from this broadcast.

"Thanks, Sam. My sources at the DEA say that an inside informant has provided critical intel to help bring down, once and for all, the cartel that moved into our area less than a year ago. Their particular brand of drugs, cut with THC secured from various sources in New Mexico and Mexico, were responsible for the uptick of drug-related deaths recently. The DEA promises to work tirelessly to get this poison off the streets. Moms and Dads, please warn your kids. Local businessman, Robert Birmingham, donated a hundred thousand dollars to start an education program against drugs. They're naming it the Samantha Anderson

Foundation in honor of a young girl who died in a local high school."

"That's my Sam!" Emerson exclaimed. "I love that. I'll have to thank Mr. Birmingham."

His Aunt Isabella and I shared a knowing look. We might have approached Robert about making amends for his recent actions by starting this foundation. Whether he did it for a tax write-off, a thank you for a second chance at life, or for some other reason, the point was that he'd done it. "I'm sure he'd love to hear that from you," Isabella answered.

The broadcast concluded.

"You weren't kidding when you said Carmen bore a likeness to you and Sydney," my mother shared.

"Yes, that's why Lester offered the solution to ID me to the police. He figured that would cover up the hit man angle. As Robert had already reported to the Diamantes that he saw me with JB earlier in the evening, they thought it wouldn't be a far stretch that she killed him. Turns out, they were about as wrong as they could be on most fronts."

"So, JB asked Lester for a boat and he refused? I thought they'd been friends for a long time," Isabella asked.

"From what I could gather from talking to Jackie after she and Lester were reunited, when JB asked for the boat, he told him he needed to get to the cove. That's where Lester had the diamonds hidden, so he thought JB was going to try and steal them. Lester refused, and JB told him he was desperate and would have no choice but to share with the authorities about all of Lester's illegal dealings, first for

CellCo by covering up their improper disposal of the batteries, then for his dealings with the cartel."

"Bad Guy One and Bad Guy Two," Kelsey added.

"Exactly. He called both bad guys after he left JB that night at The Club. The Diamantes took it from there. I still think it was Scott McIntyre who ordered the hit, or at least made the suggestion."

"We may never know," Pete added.

My phone rang. It was the same unknown caller from a week or so ago. "Excuse me, I need to take this." I moved into the kitchen. "Hello?"

"Hey, Sadie. It's Jason."

"You didn't use me for your one call, did you?"

"No, I'm actually in a safe house right now. The word on the street is I'm in jail, though. They got Little D to flip on his dad. Turns out, his father is really the brains behind the operation, and the terror. Don Seymour, Jr. was more than happy to get out from under his familial obligation. He's singing like a canary."

"That's great news. What's next for you, then? Speaking of families, I guess yours is kinda messed up now. Sorry about that."

"Yeah, well, I talked to my dad and told him the truth. Maybe if I'd done that from the beginning, things would've been different. I was trying to protect my cover, and he was trying to protect me."

"How so?" I really was curious.

"When the suggestion was floated at a meeting between unnamed individuals that the JB issue would need to be handled, they asked my father to get me to take care of it. Though I'm sure the man who mentioned it, whoever he was–"

"I'm still convinced it's Scott McIntyre, but go ahead."

"Instead of mentioning it to me, my father reached out to some of his less than desirable contacts and found the guy who did the hit. For lesser jail time, the hit man gave up my father in less than one hour of interrogation."

"Wow."

"Yeah, pretty much."

"Any news on the Romano front?" It had only been a week, but I needed to ask.

"If CellCo or the Diamantes were behind it, I haven't been able to prove it. I flat out asked my dad and he said no, but he could be lying to protect someone."

This was valid. Michael Devlyn had hired a hit man to protect his son, so lying wasn't much of a stretch at all. "I appreciate your looking into it for me."

"I'll keep trying."

"Thanks, and good luck with whatever comes next."

"You too."

I hung up the phone and returned to the living room. "Ms. Sadie?"

"Yes, Emerson?"

"I heard you mention my parents in your conversation. What's going on?"

I walked over and put my hand on his shoulder. "I thought there might be a connection between CellCo and your parents' death. I asked someone to look into it."

"And?" He had such hope in his gaze, I hated to dash it.

"And they haven't found anything yet, but they're going to keep looking."

"So am I, Emerson," Sydney added. "Sadie gave me some information and I'm going to keep working on it until we find answers for you."

He took a deep breath. "I appreciate everything you're trying to do. Auntie is right, though. At the end of the day, it won't bring them back."

"No, but we will know the truth."

"And the truth will set us free," he added with a smile.

"Amen!" My mother stood and offered her brightest smile. "Now, the truth is I worked all afternoon on tiramisu, cannolis, and crostatas, so let's have dessert."

"Yum!" came the chorus from my friends and family.

"I bought gelato. Does that count?" my father added.

"It does, Papà. It does."

Everyone except Jeremy and me made their way into the kitchen. He took my hand. "Well, you were right."

"I'm always right," I teased. "But what am I right about in particular this time?"

"Everything was connected."

"Well, almost everything. I'm not giving up."

He pulled me into a hug. "You wouldn't be Sadie Sabatini, righter of wrongs, if you did."

Smiling up at him, I decided I liked that title. "Are you good with that being my side gig?"

"I wouldn't have you any other way." And with that confession, he kissed me and made me believe all was right in the world—well, at least on our little peninsula—once again.

About the Author

USA Today Best-Selling author Nicole Leiren likes to have fun -- in life, with her characters and, of course, family and friends. A Midwesterner at heart, she now proudly calls South Texas her home and lives with her husband on a beautiful peninsula in Lake Conroe.

Nicole enjoys sharing the laughter, mystery, and occasionally a little mayhem she forces her characters to endure all for the reader's pleasure! Her stories allow you to take a break and immerse yourself in a page turning story until you reach the whodunit or happily ever after (usually both!)

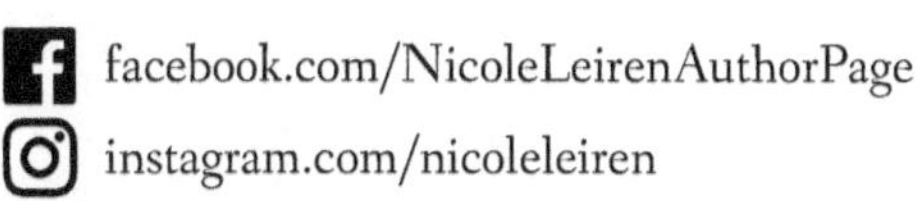

About the Publisher

Harbor Lane Books, LLC is a US-based independent digital publisher of commercial fiction, non-fiction, and poetry.

Connect with Harbor Lane Books on their website www.harborlanebooks.com and on social media @harborlanebooks.

facebook.com/harborlanebooks

x.com/harborlanebooks

instagram.com/harborlanebooks

tiktok.com/@harborlanebooks

threads.com/harborlanebooks

pinterest.com/harborlanebooks

bsky.app/profile/harborlanebooks.bsky.social

youtube.com/harborlanebooks